PRESUMPTION
OF
INNOCENCE

David Brunelle Legal Thriller #1

STEPHEN PENNER

RING OF FIRE PUBLISHING

ISBN-13: 978-0615664613
ISBN-10: 061566461X

Presumption of Innocence

Published by
Ring of Fire Publishing
Seattle, Washington, U.S.A.

Cover image by tlegend. Cover design by Stephen Penner.

A defendant is presumed innocent. This presumption continues throughout the entire trial unless during your deliberations you find it has been overcome by the evidence beyond a reasonable doubt.

State of Washington
Pattern Criminal Jury Instruction 4.01

CHAPTER 1

'Don't go inside. Call 911 and wait for the police.'

Brunelle examined the note taped to the impressive front door of the Montgomerys' suburban home. Its neatly penned letters were bathed in the red and blue strobe of the cop cars the neighbors never thought they'd see in their subdivision.

"The parents went inside, didn't they?" Brunelle asked without taking his eyes from the warning.

"Of course they did," answered Detective Chen. "The poor fools. Now they'll never get that sight out of their heads."

Brunelle shook his head. "That's too bad," he said. "You and I get paid to forget, at least once the case is over. Forget and move on to the next one."

Chen put a hand on Brunelle's shoulder. "You're gonna have trouble forgetting this one, Dave."

Brunelle frowned. He was a prosecutor with the King County Prosecutor's Office. He'd been there nearly twenty years, working his way up from shoplifting, through drug possession and burglary, to robberies and assaults, and finally homicides. He'd tried over a hundred cases and handled literally thousands more. He had to forget the details of each, at least a little bit, to be able to prosecute the next. He didn't want to get his facts mixed up in front of a jury.

But Larry Chen had been a Seattle Police officer for going on thirty years. He'd worked his way up from beat cop, to sergeant, to detective. From property crimes, through drugs and vice, to special assaults, and finally major crimes and homicides. Brunelle only saw the cases the cops could solve, but Chen saw all the ones the criminals committed. If Chen thought it was bad, it was bad.

Brunelle pushed the door open.

It was worse.

Hanging from the balcony banister at the top of the sweeping staircase that framed the palatial foyer, blocking what would otherwise have been, as designed, a breathtaking view of the perfectly decorated and immaculately clean home, was the upside-down and very lifeless body of thirteen-year-old Emily Montgomery.

"Fuck," exhaled Brunelle, the dead girl's lifeless eyes swinging grotesquely only a few feet from his own.

"Exactly," agreed Chen.

"Okay!" called out a woman from the other side of the entryway. "You can let her down now."

Brunelle watched as two patrol officers on the balcony slowly began to release the rope holding the victim aloft by her ankles. The woman who had called out to the officers stepped over to guide the body to the floor with latex-gloved hands.

Brunelle had never seen her before.

"Dave Brunelle, assistant district attorney," Chen

commenced the introductions. "This is Kat Anderson, our new assistant medical examiner."

Kat was already kneeling next to body, checking for signs of rigor. She looked up long enough to offer the quickest of hellos, then set back to her examination.

"Uh, nice to meet you," Brunelle stammered. He wondered how someone so pretty had ended up choosing cadaver-carving as a career. "I'm David."

Kat glanced up again and smiled. "Got it," she winked. "I was here when he said it."

Brunelle fought back a blush. "Right. So, uh, what did she die of?" he said to change the subject.

"Well, David Brunelle, assistant district attorney," Kat said while palpating the tissue around the girl's neck, "my thirty second diagnosis is cardiac arrest brought on by acute loss of blood."

"She bled out?" Brunelle asked doubtfully. He waved a hand around the home's entryway. "There's not a drop of blood in here."

Kat stuck a gloved finger into the linear wound in the girl's purple-white neck. "There's not a drop of blood in here either."

Brunelle frowned. He had to admit, the corpse was unusually pale. "Really?"

Kat shrugged, her finger still jutting into the lifeless neck. "Well, there's probably a few drops left, and it'll take a full autopsy to confirm it, but it looks to me like most of it's gone."

She pointed to some purple blotching just visible under the dead girl's blonde hair. "The only lividity is in the head. That means she was upside down when she died. There will be blood pooled in her head, but the rest of it left the body somehow."

"Yeah, but to where?" asked Brunelle.

"Sorry, assistant district attorney David," Kat grinned.

"That's your job."

Brunelle smiled too. "No. My job is convincing the jury the bad guy did it. But figuring out just what the bad guy did?" He slapped Chen on the back. "That's the detective's job."

"Thanks, Dave." Chen looked sideways at him. "Glad we all know our roles."

"Well, here's one thing to help you." Kat pointed to the wrists of the dead girl. There were thick lines of even whiter skin distinct in her pale flesh. "Her hands were bound when she died. This blanching means the bindings were removed after she died."

"So whoever killed her took the bindings with them," Brunelle realized.

"And apparently the blood," Kat added.

"But why?" Chen asked.

"Don't worry about why," Brunelle grinned. "I don't have to prove motive. Just who did it and how, never why."

Chen ran a hand through his hair. "Well, good. 'Cause I can't imagine any reason why anybody would do this."

Brunelle did a walk-through of the house, but didn't notice anything out of the ordinary. The forensics officers were marking, photographing, and collecting anything that might possibly hold evidentiary value. That meant casting a wide net. Brunelle wasn't looking forward to thumbing through pages upon pages of property reports containing useless enumerations of irrelevant personal property. The problem was that apart from the bloodless girl dangling in the entryway, the house was in perfect order. Better than perfect, it was slightly messy. The girl's bedroom could have used a tidying, there were a plate and cup in the sink, and the kitchen garbage needed to be taken out. Everything was as normal—and therefore as useless to him—as could be.

Time to talk to the parents. See if they could give the murder some context that was lacking in the physical evidence.

***

The parents were outside by one of the officers' patrol cars. The mother was sitting in the back of the car, its door open, her feet on the road, and a blanket around her shoulders to keep out some of the wet autumn chill that descended on Seattle after Labor Day. She was crying. Of course. The father was standing near, but not exactly next to her. He was using a cigarette to blunt the cold.

Brunelle hated talking to the family. He hated pretending that he cared. He did care, of course. Anybody would. But he didn't care that much. Not as much as someone who had known the girl. And never as much as a parent. But he was supposed to care. They always expected the cops and the prosecutors and judges and the jurors to care. But the one thing all those people really cared about was being glad it wasn't their daughter.

And in his early 40s, single, with no kids, Brunelle cared even less than that.

Besides, he knew caring wouldn't do a damn thing to bring that girl back.

"Mr. Montgomery? Mrs. Montgomery?" He stepped up with a hand half-extended. "I'm Dave Brunelle from the prosecutor's office. I'm so sorry for your loss."

Mr. Montgomery stared at Brunelle's hand but didn't shake it. He took a long drag on his cigarette. "This is death penalty, right?"

Mrs. Montgomery looked up. "Roger! This isn't the time for this."

"Really, Janet?" he replied. "Then when is? Some bastard killed your daughter and the prosecutor is standing right here."

He turned again to Brunelle. "Death penalty, right?"

Brunelle offered his professional 'no promises' smile. "Every case is different. Once the police finish their investigation, we'll review the evidence and make a decision. Your input will be very important to that decision."

"What decision?" Mr. Montgomery nearly shouted. "It's a murder. What more do you need to know?"

"Not all murders are death penalty eligible," Brunelle started. "There need to be certain aggravating factors present before—"

"Are those here?" Mr. Montgomery demanded.

"Roger, please," Mrs. Montgomery tried again.

"They might be," Brunelle was careful to answer. "As I said, we will review the evidence—"

"If the aggravating factors are there," Mr. Montgomery pressed. "Promise me you'll go after the death penalty."

Brunelle repeated the smile. "The decision isn't mine alone to make. But as I said, your input will be very important to that decision."

Mr. Montgomery was about to argue some more when Brunelle spotted Chen making his way over. "But here comes Detective Chen. I'm sure he has some questions for you."

Brunelle extracted himself as Chen approached, and quickly walked away, but not before hearing Mrs. Montgomery express her displeasure at her husband again, and Chen ask them where they had been that night while their daughter stayed home alone.

Brunelle was curious about their answer, but not curious enough to stick around. He knew he could just get it in the morning from Chen's report. Being curious wasn't the same as caring.

As he reached his car, though, he realized he was curious about more than just why the girl was home alone. He didn't have to prove motive, but damn, that was a strange way to kill someone. There must have been a reason for it. He knew if he was curious, then the jury was going to be curious too. And juries with questions are juries that acquit. So he would have to figure out that motive after all.

Then he smiled despite the weather and the circumstances. He had an excuse to call Kat.

CHAPTER 2

In the event, the call to the fetching young medical examiner had to wait. When Brunelle got into the office the next morning, the message light on his phone was already blinking. It was Chen.

"Dave, forensics got a usable print off the front door note. Ran it through the computer and came back with a possible match. I had the fingerprint people confirm it first thing this morning. Name's Holly Sandholm. Fifteen years old, but a bunch a history out at juvenile hall. We're gonna go out this morning and try to put the habeas grabus on her."

Brunelle deleted the message only to hear Chen's voice again on the next one.

"Got her, Dave. Grabbed her when she showed up for school. Heading to the precinct now. It's, uh, let's see, eight twenty-one right now. Come by if you can."

Brunelle looked at his watch. Eighty twenty-three. He turned on his heel and headed back to the elevator, pulling his cell phone out and pulling Chen's cell number up even as he pulled his overcoat back on.

***

"They're in interview room one," the officer at the reception desk said. She pressed a button behind her bulletproof glass and Brunelle heard the access door buzz and unlock. "Detective Chen said you might be stopping by."

Brunelle walked back into the offices protected behind the security door. He said hello to a couple other detectives he knew, then stepped into the observation room for interview room one. He pulled up a chair and sat down. They were just getting started.

Chen had finished reading Holly her rights and was having the girl sign the form. She looked scared. And dirty. But she wasn't as rough as some of the kids they saw. She wasn't a drug addict. Not yet anyway. All her history was property crimes and low level assaults. Typical running with the wrong crowd stuff. It was a big jump from that to murder. Especially that murder.

"Now, Holly," Chen started. "You need to understand something right from the beginning. Just because I ask you a question doesn't mean I don't already know the answer. In fact, it's just the opposite. We already know what happened and how you're involved. When I ask you something, I know the answer, but I want to see if you're going to tell me the truth or not. Does that make sense?"

Holly glanced up at Chen seated across the metal table, then to his partner, a junior detective named Jeff McCall. She looked like she was considering acting tough, but she just shrugged, and lowered her eyes back down to the tabletop. "Yeah, sure."

The girl seemed tired more than anything. She had dark bags under her eyes and her body language was someone trying to lie down even as she sat in the uncomfortable plastic chair. Brunelle figured Chen and McCall would make short work of her.

"Why don't you start at the beginning," Chen encouraged. "What brought you to Emily's house?"

Holly looked up at Chen, a strange grin on her face. She stared at him for a moment, then laughed. "You don't know shit, do you?"

Brunelle smiled and crossed his arms. Maybe this would be a good show after all.

"We know more than you think we do," Chen managed to answer. "For starters, your fingerprint is on that note."

"What note?"

"The one on the front door," McCall said. "The one you wrote."

"I didn't write it."

"We'll see what the handwriting expert says," McCall countered. "But the fingerprint is iron clad."

Holly frowned. Obviously she was weighing her choices. Brunelle just hoped she didn't ask for a lawyer. That would terminate the interview. Anything short of that they could—and would—brow beat her for however long it took.

"Your fingerprints are going to be inside too," Chen said.

Holly shook her head. "No, they won't. I'm sure about that."

"Because you wiped everything down?" McCall asked.

Holly didn't answer, which was an answer. If it was because she hadn't gone inside, she would have said as much. Silence meant that's exactly what she did. Brunelle frowned. *How would she know to do that?*

"I'm sure you did the doorknobs and the stair handrail," Chen said. "What about the toilet handle?"

Holly's brow creased.

"One thing we know, Holly, is Emily let you in," explained

Chen. "There are no signs of forced entry. The other thing we know is that you were there for a while. It takes time to kill somebody like that. So I bet you took a piss while you were there. And I bet, when you went around wiping everything down, you forgot about the shitter."

Chen's use of profanity wasn't accidental, Brunelle knew. It was designed to shake the girl just a bit. Professional cop man isn't supposed to swear. But every time he does, it distracts her a little, shoots just a little bit of adrenaline into her bloodstream, makes her a little bit more tired. Holly frowned and looked around.

Next came the bit where they drew information from the scene—like the obvious conclusion that Holly Sandholm didn't overcome Emily Montgomery by herself, or if she did, she sure as heck didn't get her tied upside down like that alone—with the ubiquitous distrust criminals have for each other. Add in a guess that a man was involved, justified by both the strength necessary and the statistical fact that most violent crime was committed by men, and the next question was ready to feed the doubt creeping into her mind.

"He told you he wiped everything down, didn't he?" asked Chen. "But I bet he forgot the toilet."

Holly's eyes shot back and forth between the detectives. "I..." But she stopped herself.

"I bet he made sure to wipe down everything *he* touched," added McCall. "They always do."

"Who always do?" Holly furled her brow.

"Well, see," Chen answered. "In something like this, there's usually the guy whose idea the whole thing was, and then there's the other person. The one who has access to the target. The one who can get him in the front door. But once the shit's gone down, the idea guy makes sure to cover up his tracks, but isn't so concerned about helping out the other person."

"That's not true," she asserted.

"We found your fingerprint on the note," McCall shrugged. "So that's already one place he forgot."

Holly's frown deepened. She looked down with wide eyes, clearly trying to decide whether to talk. So Chen hit her again.

"Whose DNA are we going to find under her fingernails, Holly?"

She looked up. "What?"

"DNA," Chen repeated. "Under her fingernails. They always take fingernail clippings and send them to the crime lab."

"And there's always DNA under the fingernails from their attacker," McCall added. "People always resist. They push and pull, and skin cells get under the fingernails. If she touched you, your DNA is on its way to the crime lab."

Holly looked at the junior detective.

He made sure she understood. "You're fucked."

"There's a way out, though," offered Chen.

Holly glared at him, her suspicion clear in her eyes.

"Look, Holly," Chen leaned onto the table, "we know this wasn't your idea. We know you never would have done this on your own."

"It's called duress," McCall explained. "And it's a complete defense. If somebody else makes you do something, you can't be held responsible for it."

Holly frowned and her eyebrows knit together. She looked down for a few moments. Then she looked up again. "What if he didn't exactly make me, but he kinda made me feel like I had to?"

"Well, uh, it's kind of a sliding scale," Chen stammered.

"Yeah, kinda depends," McCall added.

Holly's eyes widened. Her mouth shrank into a tight line.

Oh, for God's sake, thought Brunelle. He tapped on the mirror.

Chen and McCall turned around. Brunelle tapped again.

"Uh, hold on a sec, Holly." Chen stood up. "I'll be right back."

Chen stepped into the attached observation room. "Oh, Dave. You made it."

"Yeah, for all the good it's doing," Brunelle said. "Sliding scale?"

Chen rubbed the back of neck and grimaced. "Yeah, sorry. Wasn't ready for her question."

Brunelle tapped his chin for a moment. "Tell her Washington is a death penalty state."

Chen frowned. "She's a juvenile. She can't get the death penalty."

"I bet she doesn't know that," Brunelle replied. "And anyway, it's true. It is a death penalty state. But, Christ, Chen. If somebody got her to do that, he must have threatened her with a lot worse than a sliding scale. As long as she thinks what he'll do to her is worse than what you'll do to her, she'll never talk."

Chen rubbed his chin and frowned. After a moment, he nodded. "Okay, you're right. Whoever did this to her must be pretty bad news. It's worth a shot."

He slapped Brunelle on the shoulder and headed back into the interview room. He pulled out the small chair and slammed himself down onto the table.

"Holly," he started in his most sincere voice, "that was the prosecutor who's gonna handle your case. He wanted me to make sure you know Washington is a death penalty state."

Her jaw dropped almost as far as Brunelle's. He couldn't believe he told her the prosecutor was watching.

"We've been playing nice up 'til now," Chen went on. "But this is kind of it. We have other stuff to do on this case so we can't sit here all day while you try to decide what to do. I think this other guy forced you into helping him. If that's right, then you should tell us now, because no one's going to believe you later if you didn't take this opportunity to tell us now."

Holly looked from Chen to McCall. "Is this really a death penalty state?"

"I'm afraid so, Holly," McCall answered solemnly. He got what Chen was doing. "This may be your last chance."

Holly set her jaw. Her eyes narrowed. For the first time, she placed her hands on the table and folded them. She was making her decision. Brunelle hoped it was the right one. For them.

She dropped her head into her hands. "It was Arpad."

"Our pad?" asked Chen. "Whose pad? Where is —?"

"No. Arpad." Holly looked up again. This time her eyes were red rimmed. She wasn't crying yet, but almost. "A-R-P-A-D. That's his name. It's Hungarian or something. He said he was Hungarian royalty, descended from counts or something."

Brunelle winced. This wasn't good.

Chen nodded. "Okay, got it. Arpad. What's Arpad's last name?"

Holly hesitated.

"Come on, Holly," said McCall. "You've come this far."

She nodded. "All right. Karpati. Arpad Karpati." She spelled it for them.

"Do you know his birthday?" McCall asked as he scribbled the name down on his notepad. "Or at least how old he is."

"Twenty," answered Holly. "He's twenty."

Brunelle grinned. Now it *was* a death penalty case.

McCall hurried out of the room to get the suspect

information out to the detectives working the case.

"Tell me what Arpad did," Chen said.

"What he did to her?" Holly asked, as her eyes finally released a tear. "Or what he did to me?"

CHAPTER 3

Brunelle leaned forward. This might turn out to be more than just a death penalty case. Holly was fifteen. Karpati was twenty. And since they were more than forty eight months apart... but he decided to stop his suppositions, and wait to see what she actually said.

"What did he do to you, Holly?" Chen asked. If he wasn't sincerely concerned for her, he sure sounded like he was.

"He, well, that is." She put a hand up to her eyes. "It's just that. Well, see, he was my boyfriend, and..."

"Understood," said Chen. "Did he force you to have sex?"

Holly nodded, but couldn't manage any words.

"Okay, Holly, why don't we come back to that?" It was interesting and important—and criminal even without force—but if she wasn't really ready to talk about it, it could end up derailing the entire interrogation. "Let's talk about Emily. Tell me what Arpad did to the girl."

Holly nodded. Then she did. The whole story. Brunelle listened intently. Chen and he both wanted the information, but it had very different value to each of them. Everything she told Chen could be used against Karpati to make the case against him and justify his arrest. And everything she told Chen would be completely inadmissible against Karpati at trial because it would be hearsay.

Unless Holly went from defendant to witness. Which meant explaining to those parents why the girl who helped murder their daughter and hang her from the balcony was getting a sweetheart deal to turn State's evidence and walk away with a slap on the wrist.

Holly had met Karpati at a club. He was older and cool and dark and edgy. He chatted her up. They danced, they drank, they fucked. She thought he was the best thing ever. He seemed to be able to tolerate her. His disdain just made her want him more. She wanted to know all his secrets. He told her she didn't want that, she couldn't handle it. She insisted. He told her he was descended from vampires. He didn't need blood like real vampires. Not every day. But he did need it sometimes. And it had to be pure blood. Girl's blood. Virgin's blood.

That had hurt her. She wasn't a virgin. Hadn't been since some boy in seventh grade. She couldn't help him. But then again, maybe she could. She had friends. Girls she'd met here and there. Most had lived lives like her, but there were a few, the snooty girls with the rich parents she met through the church where her probation officer said she could do her community service hours. Girls like Emily Montgomery.

So she told Karpati about Emily and they hatched a plan. Holly chatted her up and made friends. Waited for her to mention a time she'd be home alone. It didn't take long and soon enough they had a day picked out. They parked in Karpati's car down the street, lights dimmed, and waited for Emily's parents to leave. Then they drove up and parked a few houses away. Holly knocked and Emily opened the door. Of course she did. She knew Holly.

But she didn't know the man who stepped from the shadows and pushed her back inside by her throat. The man who overpowered her and bound her hands behind her back. The man who suspended her upside down, then slit her throat and collected the spurting blood into a bucket while Holly vomited in the bathroom.

She had insisted on leaving the note for the parents. Karpati had argued with her, told her it was stupid and soft and sentimental, but she had insisted. He stormed off to the car while she scrawled out the message, her back to the girl swinging slowly behind her.

Karpati hadn't said a word the drive back to his apartment. When they got there he told her it was better they slept separate that night. In case they were followed, he said. And besides, she didn't want to see what he was going to do with the blood.

He was right. She didn't.

She tried to go to school the next day but the cops grabbed her as she headed toward the building. And now here she was.

When she finished, Holly looked up and shrugged. "Do you believe me?"

Chen nodded. "I believe you."

Brunelle wasn't so sure.

***

"So she didn't do *anything*?" Brunelle challenged Chen as Holly waited in the interrogation room.

"People always minimize their own role," Chen shrugged. "Besides that's enough for accessory to murder."

"Of course it is," Brunelle answered. "She picked out the victim and got her to open the door. All with knowledge of what this Karpati guy had planned."

Brunelle frowned and shook his head. "But I don't buy it. She was in deeper than what she's claiming."

"So what? It's enough to convict her."

"I don't want to convict *her*," Brunelle explained. "I want to convict him. I believe her when she says it was his idea and he's a fucking psychopath. But I need the jury to believe her too."

Chen furrowed his brow at Brunelle. "If you're gonna cut her a deal to testify, isn't it better if she says she didn't do anything?"

"It is if she's telling the truth. But if her story is bullshit, and the forensics comes back to prove it, then she's worthless. If she says she never touched Emily, but it's her DNA on the fingernail clippings? If she says she didn't hoist the body up, but they find her fingerprints on the balcony railing?"

Chen nodded. "Yeah, okay. I see your point."

"Go back in and see if she won't give you something more," Brunelle instructed. "But don't mention me this time. If she won't give you the whole story now, she'll give it to me later when I tell her lawyer she's gotta come clean to get a deal. We may not be able to execute her, but we can damn well put her in prison for the better part of her life."

CHAPTER 4

It took several days to locate Karpati. With a name like Arpad Karpati it wasn't hard to find his address, but the guy knew the cops would be looking for him, so he wasn't staying there any more. The stake out of his apartment only confirmed he had abandoned it.

But he still liked the girlies.

Holly had given them the name of the night club they had met at. "Darkness." According to Chen it was frequented by whatever had become of the goth craze. Lots of black clothes, black eyeliner, and black pills. The name had led to a photograph which had led to an arrest outside the club a few days later.

"We got 'im," Chen said when Brunelle answered his cell phone during Thursday night football.

"On my way."

"Main precinct. Twenty minutes."

This time Brunelle was already waiting in the observation

room when they brought Karpati in.

He looked like a real jerk.

Tall and gaunt, but with broad shoulders and large hands. He kept his hair short and sported deep acne scars over both cheeks. His thin lips were locked in a sneer as McCall sat him down opposite Chen. They didn't take his cuffs off.

"Do you know why you're here, Arpad?" Chen started.

Brunelle loved that question. If they said yes, it was practically a confession. If they said no, well, then Chen had them lying from the outset. He waited to see how Arpad Karpati would answer.

"Why don't you tell me?"

Brunelle frowned. That was a pretty damn good response. He hoped Chen could get somewhere with this guy.

"I think you know why, Arpad," Chen said. "So why don't we cut right to the chase. We know you killed Emily Montgomery. We know how you did it and we know why you did it. So make this easy on yourself. We just want to hear your side of the story."

Karpati tipped his head back and appraised the detectives opposite him. He set his jaw, but his lip started to quiver.

"Detective Chen was it?" he asked shakily.

"Yes. Chen."

"What's your first name, Detective Chen?" The lip quavered visibly.

Chen hesitated. "Larry. Detective Larry Chen."

Karpati offered a tight smile. "Thank you, Larry."

He raised his cuffed hands to his face and wiped at his eyes. "I want you to believe me when I say this, Larry."

Chen leaned forward. So did Brunelle.

'It's very important that you understand what I'm about to tell you."

"We'll understand, Arpad," Chen assured. McCall nodded.

Brunelle wondered whether this guy really was a nut job. Maybe they'd be looking at an insanity plea.

Karpati lowered his hands. "Good," he whispered. "Thank you, Larry."

He nodded, his face looking as solemn as a vicar at a funeral, and said, "Then please believe me when I tell you. Please understand when I say...."

Then the face melted into a hateful grin, "That I want a lawyer."

Karpati threw himself back in his chair and laughed. When he looked at the awestruck detectives again, he laughed even harder.

Chen slammed himself to his feet. "Get this bastard out of my sight. Book him on murder one."

McCall jerked him to his feet. "Does this mean you don't want to talk to me?" Karpati taunted as McCall dragged him from the room.

Chen paced for a moment then punched the table. "Damn it!"

Brunelle walked into the interrogation room. He couldn't keep from smiling.

"Okay," he said. "You have to admit, that was pretty funny."

"Fuck you." Chen was angry but he started to laugh too. "Damn it. That fucker got me."

"He sure did. It was looking good for a minute there."

Chen slapped the table one more time. "Well, when the jury sees that, they'll know what an asshole he is."

Brunelle shook his head. "No, they won't see that. We can never tell a jury that somebody asked for a lawyer. It's an improper comment on his right to remain silent."

Chen's eyes widened. "It's not just that he asked for a lawyer. Hell, they ask for lawyers all the time. It's how he asked for it. Playing me like that, like this is all some fucking game. Can't that come in?"

Brunelle pursed his lips. "It might. Maybe. If I could convince a judge it was distinct enough from the request. Maybe sanitize it a bit. But I'm not gonna do that."

"Why not?" Brunelle could see Chen was still angry.

"Because, that's exactly the little detail, the little something extra, the envelope pushing, chalk on the shoes kinda overreaching that appellate courts use to overturn convictions on death cases."

Chen's scowl gave way to a smile. "So this is going to be a death case?"

"Oh yes," replied Brunelle. "We're gonna kill that son of a bitch."

CHAPTER 5

"Jessica Edwards," answered Holly's public defender when she picked up the phone.

"Jess, it's Dave," said Brunelle. "Let's talk deal."

"Why, I'm fine today, Dave," Jessica replied. "And how are you?"

Brunelle took a deep breath and allowed himself a smile. "I'm fine, Jess. Thanks for asking. Did you sleep well last night?"

"That, David Brunelle, is none of your damn business."

Brunelle had to laugh. He was tempted to follow up with a 'What was his name?' but thought better of it. They were too close in age and both too single for that kind of talk to be anything but regrettable. Instead he got back to business.

"Holly Sandholm. Is she interested in testifying against her boyfriend? He was arrested this morning."

"Yeah, I heard about it. It's all over the news."

"So, is she on board?" Brunelle pressed. He knew he needed

her testimony to explain what happened inside the house. Jessica knew it too.

"Well, that brings up an interesting point," she said, "since she's also a victim."

Brunelle considered. "The child rape?"

"Yup. Did you check their birthdates yet? He's four years and two months older than her. Rape of a Child in the Third Degree."

Brunelle nodded as he pulled the statute up on his computer. "Okay," he started. "Honestly, I'm a little more interested in the murder."

"I figured you would be," answered Jess. "That's why I checked the birthdates myself. Charge the bastard with that too and she's on board."

Brunelle tapped his chin. "I can probably do that. It's going to complicate things."

"Our stuff is always complicated."

Brunelle frowned. "You want it to be, but I don't. I want straight forward. Bad guy does bad thing. He's guilty. The end."

"Dave?" said Jessica.

"Yeah?"

"That's not real life."

Brunelle pursed his lips. "Okay, let me review the reports again. We're gonna arraign him tomorrow morning."

"Thanks, Dave."

"And Jess?"

"Yeah, Dave?"

"I know why you really want me to add that charge. If I do, they can't be tried together. And if they're gonna be separate trials, then it's way more likely she gets to stay in juvenile court where she'll get a slap on the wrist no matter what she's convicted of."

"Mr. Brunelle!" Jess laughed. "I am shocked—shocked, I say— that you would think that."

"But I'm right, aren't I?"

Jess laughed again. "Of course you are. But I didn't think you'd figure it out so quick."

Brunelle laughed a bit too. "I'll call you before I leave the office tonight. Let you know what we decide."

"We?"

"I can't seek death without the boss' approval," Brunelle explained. "I'm meeting with Duncan in half an hour."

Jess chuckled. "Wow. Good luck with that."

"Thanks," Brunelle said. "I'll need it."

***

"Dave! Come in!"

Matt Duncan, elected prosecuting attorney for King County, was amazingly friendly. He knew everybody, and made everybody feel like they were the only person in the world right then. He was a politician more than a prosecutor, which suited Brunelle fine. The office needed a well-connected politician in charge when dealing with the county council on budget matters and civic groups on crime prevention. But it led to some ass-backwards decision making sometimes. Brunelle really hoped this wouldn't be one of those times.

"Thanks, Matt." Brunelle took a chair across Duncan's desk. Duncan was astute enough to have a regular desk, nice one, bigger than most, but still government issue. He was a public servant after all. And he usually did his press conferences in his office.

"So," Duncan got right to it. "You want to go death, I take it?"

"Have you seen the crime scene photos?" Brunelle asked in reply. "Hell yes, I want to go death."

Duncan frowned. "How strong is the evidence? I don't want to seek death if we're not going to get it. It's all about expectations."

Brunelle wanted to counter, 'I thought it was all about justice,' but he knew better.

"It's solid. His accomplice wants to testify against him."

"So cut one killer a deal to get death on the other?" Duncan considered. "Jury's not gonna like that. They're not going to impose the death penalty on one if the other isn't getting it."

"The other isn't eligible. She's fifteen."

Duncan nodded. "Okay, that helps."

"And he raped her. The codefendant," Brunelle clarified. "Not the victim."

"Raped her?"

"Well, statutory rape," Brunelle explained. "He's more than forty-eight months older than her."

"Still," Duncan rubbed his chin. "It explains the disparity in treatment. What are the aggravators?"

Brunelle frowned. This was the hard part.

"There are three I think might apply," Brunelle started. "Committed during the course of a burglary. Deliberate cruelty to the victim rising to the level of torture. And um," he hesitated, "committed to maintain or elevate status in an identifiable group."

"The gang aggravator?" Duncan looked sideways at Brunelle.

"Well yeah. That's what everybody calls it, but it has wider application than that."

Duncan's eyes narrowed. "Let's start with the burglary. Did they steal something from the house?"

"Doesn't look like it," Brunelle admitted.

"So how is there a burglary?"

"Well," Brunelle smiled, "burglary is unlawful entering with intent to commit any crime. Murder is a crime."

"So you're going to bootstrap the murder to aggravate itself?"

Brunelle shrugged. "You say that like it's a bad thing."

Duncan smirked. "What else you got?"

"Deliberate cruelty to the level of torture."

Duncan raised an eyebrow. "Did they do that?"

"Depends on your definition of torture," answered Brunelle. "They bound her hands, hung her upside down, and slit her throat."

"Not to diminish the tragedy here, Dave, but that doesn't sound like torture. In fact, I think that's the so-called humane way of killing animals so the meat is kosher."

"Well, I'll let the defense attorney argue that it was humane," Brunelle replied. "We're not animals. That girl knew what was happening to her."

Duncan shifted in his seat. "What's the last one? The gang one? What's the identifiable group he's trying to elevate himself in?"

Brunelle grimaced. If Duncan had disliked the other aggravators, he was going to hate this one.

"Vampires."

Duncan waited for a minute, perhaps hoping it was a joke.

"Seriously," added Brunelle.

Duncan leaned onto his desk. "Look, Dave. Everybody thinks I'm gonna run for governor one of these days. But you know what? I'm not. Who needs that crap? Roads and schools and parks and prisons and everything else under the God damn sun. No, I got it good here. Bring justice to the community, give some speeches, and I've been doing it so long, no one even files to run against me anymore."

He leaned back into his chair again. "I let you charge that, I'll be looking for a new job next election day."

Brunelle knew Duncan was right. He was grasping at straws. This had to be a death case. Or at least life without parole. But if they couldn't prove one of those aggravating factors, Karpati could get away with only twenty years. He'd only be forty when he got out. That wasn't justice.

"I think the torture one is your best bet," Duncan said. "I'll let you go capital, but not on vampires. You'll need to prove that what they did was torture."

Brunelle bit his cheek and nodded. "Arraignment's first thing tomorrow."

"Then you'd better get moving, Dave, and figure out how to make that stick. You'll need an expert."

Brunelle smiled. "I know just who to talk to."

CHAPTER 6

"Dr. Anderson?" Brunelle rapped on the assistant medical examiner's office door. It was right off the examining room at the morgue. Brunelle supposed if it didn't bother her to stick her hands into decomposing bodies, she probably didn't even think about having her office near the examining room.

Kat was sitting at her small desk, typing something into her computer. She turned around at the knock.

"Why, if it isn't David Brunelle, Assistant District Attorney." She smiled. A bright, full lipped smile. "What brings you to my humble office?"

Brunelle tried not to stare at her pretty mouth, but it only led to his eyes dropping to her curvy body. He looked away, at some gruesome autopsy photographs on her desk, and was able to gather himself again.

"The Montgomery murder," Brunelle managed to say. "I need to pick your brain a bit."

Kat laughed. "You know, I actually do pick brains. Real ones. Part of the job."

Brunelle smiled. Medical examiners were weird. They had to be. Who else could do that job? He just hadn't met one so beautiful before. So, ironically, alive.

"Ha. Yeah. Medical examiner humor," said Brunelle. "I'll have to come by and observe sometime."

Kat tipped her head. "You'd do that?"

Brunelle shrugged. "For the right case. I've been to a few over the years."

Kat stuck out her lip and nodded. "That's impressive, David Brunelle. So what can I do for you on the Montgomery homicide?"

"Murder," Brunelle insisted.

"Murder is a legal term," Kat answered. "That's your job. Mine is medical. It was a homicide. You get to prove it was murder."

"Then help me do that," Brunelle replied.

Kat crossed her arms. "Not really my job, David. But what do you need to know?"

"Did you confirm she bled out?" Brunelle started.

"Oh yes. No doubt about that. The typical body usually has about five or six liters of blood. She lost at least two liters. Maybe two and a half. There was no other trauma, so that's definitely the cause of death."

"She did have that incision on her neck," Brunelle pointed out.

"Right," Kat smiled and pointed a finger at him. "I said *other* trauma.' Don't try to trick me, lawyer-man. That laceration was the only pathology on the body. It was the exit for the blood, and the lack of blood caused her heart to stop."

"Did it hurt?" Brunelle asked.

Kat nodded. "I imagine it did. A cut to your neck is going to hurt."

Brunelle shook his head. "No, not the cut. The bleeding out. Would that have hurt?"

Kat considered. "Not really, I wouldn't think. The cut was to the carotid artery. Clean, exact cut. I mean, really, whoever did this had an excellent grasp of anatomy. I couldn't have picked a better place for the incision."

"Wow, that's great, Dr. Anderson," said Brunelle. "Maybe tone the professional admiration down a bit for the jury when you testify though, okay?"

Kat frowned. "It's not admiration. I'm simply explaining that whoever made this cut knew exactly where to cut to cause the most amount of blood to be ejected from the body until her heart stopped beating. And even then, it would have dripped and drained a bit."

Brunelle was used to having to bring witnesses back around to the answer he needed. "And so that sensation, of your blood pumping out of your neck with each heart beat—would that have been painful? Or better yet, excruciating?"

Kat let out a surprised laugh. "Excruciating is better?"

Brunelle shrugged. "Lawyer thing."

"I guess so," Kat raised an eyebrow and looked away. "Well, no. Definitely not excruciating. And probably not terribly painful either. Terrifying, but not painful."

Brunelle frowned and tapped absently on the doorframe. "Well, that's too bad."

"Too bad that the girl didn't endure excruciating pain?" Kat asked.

Brunelle shrugged again. "Like I said, lawyer thing.

"I knew I didn't like lawyers," Kat joked.

Brunelle raised an eyebrow. "We're not all bad. And besides I'm not really a lawyer, I'm a prosecutor."

"Is there a difference?"

"I think there is."

Kat nodded. "You keep telling yourself that, David. Maybe you'll convince yourself."

Brunelle laughed, but more out of politeness. His mind was already considering the possibilities.

"Can I come pick your brain again," he asked, "if I think of any other questions?"

Kat smiled and crossed her shapely legs. "You can pick my brain anytime, David Brunelle. But next time, let's do it over coffee."

Brunelle's eyebrows shot up. He didn't say anything for a moment.

"A speechless lawyer," she laughed. "That's a rare sight."

Brunelle smiled. "I always get quiet when I'm happy. Thanks, Dr. Anderson."

"Call me Kat."

"I will," Brunelle stepped back in to the hallway. "I promise."

CHAPTER 7

The arraignment was scheduled for nine o'clock. The camera crews were already lined up outside the courtroom. Brunelle was looking over the charging documents in his office when there came a knock on his door.

It was Duncan. "You all set?" he asked.

Brunelle nodded. "I think so."

"No vampires, right?"

Brunelle laughed. "Right. No vampires. Burglary and torture."

"Think you can make those stick?"

Brunelle recalled the dead girl's face hanging upside down in front of him as he entered the home that night. "Yeah. Pretty sure I can."

Duncan grinned. "Good. Now let's just hope he gets a shitty lawyer."

Brunelle smiled again. "Sure. But not too shitty. I don't want it to come back on ineffective assistance of counsel."

"Good point," said Duncan. Then, tapping his chin, he added. "When you finish with the arraignment, stop by and we can talk about a second chair."

"Second chair?" Brunelle repeated. "I figured I'd try it alone. I don't need co-counsel."

Duncan shrugged slightly. "Oh, it might be a good idea. Chance for somebody to learn from you. Besides, it's always good to have another set of eyes look at something."

Brunelle nodded, but he wasn't excited about having to take time to teach a junior attorney how to try a death case. But he could worry about that after the arraignment.

"Okay, I'll stop by. Maybe we'll even know who his lawyer is by then."

***

"William Harrison Welles," said the dapper man with the expensive suit and graying ponytail. He was addressing the semi-circle of reporters who had pinned him against the wall, their camera lights beaming and microphone extended. "And I am proud to be representing Mr. Karpati."

Brunelle stopped in his tracks when he saw Welles. *Damn it,* he thought. Not only was Welles not a shitty attorney, he was a really damn good attorney. Worse, he was a media-loving publicity hound of an attorney who had reached semi-celebrity status in Seattle for defending some of the higher profile cases in the last few years.

But he was expensive. Brunelle wondered whether Karpati could really afford him, or Welles was just using this as more free publicity.

"Mr. Karpati is an innocent man," Welles went on. "He has been unjustly accused based on the unreliable word of a fifteen year-old juvenile delinquent, whom the State knows cannot be believed."

Brunelle clenched his fists. Welles could say whatever he wanted, and there would be no repercussions. He was a defense attorney, sworn to use every available trick in the trade to defeat the State's allegations. But if Brunelle said anything more than confirming the charges and a general, 'We believe the evidence supports the charge,' then he was looking at a bar complaint or worse. Because then he would be trying to prejudice the defendant's right to a fair trial.

Welles wasn't saying Karpati was innocent because he was. He was saying that psychopathic murderer was innocent because the twelve people who would eventually be sitting on the jury, months from now, whoever they might end up being—at least some of them would be watching the news tonight. And in the back of their mind, one or two might remember thinking at the time they heard the first news reports about it, 'Didn't somebody say he was innocent? Accused by some fifteen year old liar?'

Brunelle squeezed his file and began walking again toward the arraignment courtroom. A couple of the reporters saw him and broke off to get a comment from him.

"We believe the evidence supports the charge," Brunelle said into the blinding glare of the camera.

"Is it true your case is based on the word of a fifteen year old juvenile delinquent?"

Brunelle managed a tight smile. "I'll have copies of the charging documents after the arraignment." And he pushed through them into the courtroom.

Welles had slipped inside during the paparazzi assault on Brunelle and was opening his Italian leather briefcase on the defense counsel table.

"Nice to see you again, Dave," he said. "Better luck this time."

Brunelle grimaced. "Nice to see you too. And thanks." He recalled the last case he and Welles had tried together. Welles had gotten an acquittal with a strange hybrid defense of prescription drug abuse, self defense, and baseless police misconduct allegations. "You know that guy killed somebody three months after you got him off, right?"

Welles shrugged. "Don't worry Dave. He paid his bill in full before he went back to prison."

Nice, thought Brunelle. "So is this one pro bono?"

Welles smiled. "There are two things I never do, Dave. One is discuss fees. The other is handle a case for free."

"This guy has that kind of money?" Brunelle was surprised. Welles was top tier, and charged top tier money. But more than surprised, Brunelle was really fishing for information.

Welles didn't bite. "As I said, I never discuss fees." He put out a hand. "Do you have copies of the charging paperwork for my client?"

Brunelle pulled the forms from his file and handed them to his adversary. "I'll let the judicial assistant know we're ready."

A few minutes later, Judge Quinn took the bench.

"All rise!" announced the judicial assistant. "The King County Superior Court is now in session. The Honorable Susan Quinn presiding."

"You may be seated," said the judge as she took her seat above the litigants. "Are the parties ready on the matter of the State of Washington versus Arpad Karpati?"

"The State is ready," answered Brunelle.

"May it please the court," said Welles. "William Harrison Welles entering my notice of appearance on behalf of my client, Mr.

Karpati. We are ready to enter our plea of not guilty and begin our vigorous defense of these false accusations."

Judge Quinn stared down at Welles for several seconds. "Save it for the jury, Mr. Welles. I just need to know if we can bring your client in."

Welles smiled. "By all means, Your Honor."

The judge nodded to the guards, who opened a side door to the holding cells built behind the courtrooms. Karpati strutted in, hands cuffed in front of him and a guard right behind him. He was wearing his jail-issued gray pajamas and plastic flip-flops. He grinned at the gallery and shook, as best he could, Welles' hand.

"May my client be unhandcuffed, Your Honor?" Welles requested. "I assure you he poses no threat to anyone."

Judge Quinn nodded again and one of the guards stepped over to unhandcuff Karpati. Then the guard directed him by the shoulders into the defendant's chair at the defense table. Welles sat beside him and put his arm around him, whispering something in his ear. Brunelle stayed up at the bar and handed the charging documents to the judicial assistant, who passed them to the judge.

"At this time," began Brunelle, "the State is filing charges of Aggravated Murder in the First Degree against Mr. Karpati."

That much was on the first page. Brunelle was pretty sure Welles hadn't looked at page two yet.

"In addition," Brunelle went on, "the State is filing a count of Rape of a Child in the Third Degree."

That got Karpati's attention. He surrendered an agitated "What?!" before Welles grabbed his arm and whispered something in his ear. Whatever Welles said didn't seem to make Karpati any less angry, but he didn't say anything more.

Welles stood up. "We have received copies of the charging documents, Your Honor. We waive a formal reading of the charges, and enter pleas of absolutely not guilty to all counts."

Brunelle rolled his eyes at the 'absolutely.'

"We would like," Welles went on, "to be heard on conditions of release pending trial."

Brunelle had already pre-filled out the order on conditions of release. Aggravated murder in the first degree was a capital offense. The court always held capital defendants in custody without the opportunity to post bail. Nevertheless, the judge looked at Brunelle. "What is the State's recommendation as to conditions of release?"

Brunelle, still dumbstruck by even the request to discuss bail, hesitated before replying. "Uh, we would ask the court to hold Mr. Karpati without bail. This is a capital case, and pursuant to the state constitution, capital defendants are not entitled to bail."

The judge turned to the defense attorney. "Mr. Welles, what say you? It is the normal practice of this court to hold capital defendants without bail."

"It may be, Your Honor," Welles said with a flourish of his hand, "but only because I have yet to argue this issue before this court."

Brunelle resisted his urge to huff, and instead busied himself by pretending to take notes on Welles' argument. Judge Quinn raised an eyebrow, but didn't interrupt.

"The State constitution does not deny a capital defendant his Constitutional right to bail," Welles went on. He pulled out a green covered statute book from his large brief case. He flipped it open to the page he had already bookmarked. "It merely makes such assurance explicit for noncapital cases. The actual language is, and I quote, 'All persons charged with a crime shall be bailable by sufficient sureties, except for capital offenses when the proof is evident or presumption great.'"

Brunelle looked askance at Welles. The judge did the same. "That doesn't seem to support your position, Mr. Welles," she said.

"Oh, but it does, Your Honor," Welles smiled. "Listen again. 'All persons charged with a crime shall be bailable.' All. The only exception is capital offenses. But not all capital offenses. Oh no. Only those where the proof is evident or the presumption great. Well, we know what the presumption is. My client is presumed innocent. The presumption is great, your honor, in fact it is sacrosanct. But it is a presumption of innocence and therefore a presumption of bail."

"What about the part about the proof being evident?" Judge Quinn asked.

"Precisely!" Welles threw a hand in the air. "What about that evident proof? Where is it? Is it here today? Has the State brought anyone to present this evident proof? No, of course not. Because my client is innocent. Innocent, I say. And I daresay they know that, and that is why they have not brought any evidence to today's hearing. Just some flimsy pieces of paper drafted by the prosecutor this morning. There is no proof in this case, Your Honor. None. And therefore, under the constitution of this great State, you, Your Honor, with all due respect, you are absolutely prohibited from denying my client bail."

Judge Quinn let her stare linger at Welles for a minute. Then she pursed her lips and looked at Brunelle. "State's response?"

"The State has filed a criminal complaint," Brunelle responded evenly, "which charges the defendant with the crime of aggravated murder in the first degree. That is a capital offense. Attached to the complaint is a summary of the investigation which includes information from an eyewitness that the defendant committed the crime in her presence. The proof is evident. The court should deny bail."

"The eyewitness," Welles laughed, "is a fifteen-year-old drug addict, with a history of lying to the police, whose fingerprints were found at the scene and who has every reason to claim someone else did it. In addition, she is currently charged in juvenile as a codefendant, and therefore cannot be called as a witness by the State at my client's trial without violating her Fifth Amendment right to remain silent. The police officers will not be permitted to testify as to what she said, because that would be hearsay and would deny my client his Sixth Amendment right to confront the witnesses against him, mainly this lying little miscreant. There is absolutely no admissible evidence against my client and the first thing I will be doing after this hearing is drafting up my motion to dismiss this case."

The judge looked back to Brunelle. "Is the girl charged out at juvenile hall with this murder?"

"She is, Your Honor," Brunelle admitted. "However, I have already had negotiations with her attorney and I have a good faith belief that she will be available to testify at Mr. Karpati's trial. In fact, Your Honor, the girl in question is the victim of count two, the rape of child in the third degree, so the State has already been contemplating needing to call her as a witness for that count."

Judge Quinn nodded as she considered the arguments.

"You Honor, if I may respond?" Welles tried, but she waved him off.

"No. Mr. Welles, thank you. I believe I understand your argument. I also believe it has some merit. We regularly set no-bail holds on capital defendants, but I hadn't really thought about that evident proof requirement until you argued it just now."

She tapped her lips in thought.

"Here's what we're going to do. I am going to rule that the State must present evident proof before I can deny bail."

Brunelle clenched his jaw, but didn't say anything.

"I'm also going to find that they haven't done that here today. I think an affidavit from the prosecutor can be enough, but not if the evidence comes from a witness who might be unavailable at trial."

"Your Honor—" Brunelle tried, but Judge Quinn shushed him as well.

"Sorry, Mr. Brunelle. You've had your chance to speak. We will schedule a hearing in one week. I will give the State a chance to present this evident proof. It can be done in affidavit form by the prosecutor. You don't need to bring live witnesses in, Mr. Brunelle. That's what the trial is for. But any witness you reference in the affidavit had better be available as of next week. That means you better get that deal worked out with the girl before the bail hearing, or I'm liable to find there is not evident proof to justify a no bail hold. Do you understand?"

Unfortunately, Brunelle did.

"In the meantime, I will allow bail."

"Thank you, Your Honor," said Welles. "We would ask the court to set a minimal amount, perhaps five thousand—"

"Ten million dollars," announced Judge Quinn. "It's still a capital case, Mr. Welles, evident proof or not."

Welles was about to argue, but then thought better of it. "Yes, Your Honor. Thank you, Your Honor."

"Anything else, Mr. Brunelle?"

"No, Your Honor."

"Then this matter is concluded," the judge declared. "We will see you back here in one week, ready to argue bail and any other matters duly noted."

Judge Quinn stood up and stepped out as the judicial assistant instructed everyone to stand again.

"Nice argument," Brunelle whispered to Welles as he collected up his things.

"Wait until next week, Dave," Welles whispered back.

CHAPTER 8

"You have reached the voicemail of Jessica Edwards of the King County Public Defender's Office. Please leave a message and I will call you back as soon as possible. If you are a client and currently detained in the King County Jail, press zero to speak with the receptionist."

"Jess, it's Dave," Brunelle said into his phone even as Duncan darkened his door and gave him the charades version of 'come to my office when you hang up.' "Just calling to firm up the deal with Holly. A little unexpected change of plans this morning. I need to have this in place by next week. Call me."

Then he hung and walked the short distance from his nice office to Duncan's very nice office.

"Heard what happened this morning," Duncan said as Brunelle stepped in and sat down.

"Yeah, that kind of sucked. But I'm pretty sure he won't post ten million."

"He only needs ten percent to get a bonding company to do

it for him," Duncan observed.

"That's still a million cash. And he wouldn't get it back at the end. But it doesn't matter because I'll get that no bail hold next week. Just need the get the girl signed up."

Duncan frowned, then nodded. "I'm sure you're right. Now have you given any thought to a co-counsel?"

Brunelle shook his head. "No, not yet. I was trying to think of someone who could use the experience but wouldn't get in my way."

"What about Yamata?" Duncan suggested.

"Michelle Yamata?" Brunelle confirmed. "Uh, well. I've heard good things about her."

He'd heard bad things too. Like she filed a harassment complaint against her last employer, one of the boutique litigation firms in town, and left as part of the settlement. Brunelle didn't want to be anywhere near her.

"Do you think she's ready?" Brunelle questioned. "I know there are some more senior attorneys who haven't had the chance yet to work on a capital c—"

"She's ready," asserted Duncan. "And she's better than those other attorneys."

She was also far more attractive. Duncan had a penchant for hiring the most attractive job applicant. Yamata, a tall leggy Japanese-American woman, was certainly one of his more attractive hires. She was also at least ten years younger than Brunelle and would, as co-counsel, be in exactly the type of position to him that would support another claim.

"Can I think about it?" Brunelle asked.

"Not any more," Duncan smiled and stood up. "Michelle, thanks for coming."

Brunelle turned and saw Yamata standing in the doorway.

She was wearing a burgundy power suit and dark stockings with the suggestion of a fishnet design. Brunelle managed to smile as he extended a hand.

"Welcome aboard, partner," he said.

Yamata shook his hand strongly. "Thanks. But welcome aboard what?"

Her voice was deeper than Brunelle would have expected. It bothered him that he even noticed. He was really going to have to be careful.

"Dave?" Duncan punted Yamata's question to him. Brunelle smiled anyway.

"I need a second chair," Brunelle started, then opted for more equal terminology, "that is, co-counsel for a capital case I just filed."

"Capital?" confirmed Yamata. "As in death? Oh yeah, I'm on board. Can I shove the needle in his arm?"

She laughed a deep, throaty laugh.

Brunelle wasn't sure what to think. He was pretty sure he was scared.

But he kind of liked her attitude too.

"When do I start?" she asked.

"Right now," declared Duncan. "Why don't you go down the hall to Dave's office and he'll brief you on the case."

"Great," said Yamata. "I know where your office is." And she started down the hallway, her tight ass swinging invitingly down the hall.

Brunelle turned from the sight and forced a smile to Duncan. "Thanks, boss."

Duncan winked. "I knew you'd approve. Go get her, tiger."

Brunelle nodded, but the smile slid from his face as he turned and followed his new partner to his office.

***

She was sitting in his chair. "Nice view," she motioned toward his windows and Elliot Bay beyond. "I have an interior office in the drug unit."

She popped up and danced to one of the chairs across his desk. "I can't wait to work on a murder case. I'm so sick of drug possession trials. Two rocks, two cops, two days. I want something I can really sink my teeth into."

She leaned forward as Brunelle sat in his chair. It smelled of her perfume. She had really nice perfume.

"Just tell me what to do, Mr. Brunelle. I'll do anything you say. Anything."

Brunelle succeeded in forcing out the improper thoughts that rushed toward his mind's eye. Instead, he said, "Let's start with not calling me 'Mr. Brunelle.' That makes me feel old. 'Dave' will be fine."

Yamata smiled, a bright, full-lipped, red-lipstick smile. "Okay, Dave. So, what do I do first?"

"First," said Brunelle. "You listen."

Then he pulled the binder of scene and autopsy photographs off of his bookshelf and slid it across the desk to her. "And follow along."

So he told her the facts of the case. Everything from Holly's fingerprint on the note to Karpati's high-priced asshole defense attorney. She had tried to follow along in the binder, but couldn't quite make it through all the photographs. When he'd finished, he asked, "Any questions?"

Yamata paused, then answered, "Yeah, one."

"What is it?"

"Seriously," she said, "Can I shove the needle in his arm?"

Brunelle appreciated her enthusiasm. "Sorry, no. There's a

separation of powers thing or something. But let's take it one step at a time. We have to get a conviction first."

Yamata grinned. "Right. First thing's first."

But that reminded Brunelle of what really came first. "Actually, the first thing we have to do is lock in his accomplice as our witness."

Then he explained what had happened that morning.

"Wow, that sucks," Yamata observed. "Hope he doesn't bail out before then."

"Well, I don't think he will," Brunelle answered. "But even if he does, the judge will take him back into custody if we can show her he has to be held without bail."

"Need a brief?" Yamata offered. "My briefs are exquisite."

Brunelle nodded. "Of course they are."

Then he shook the thoughts of her panties—her exquisite panties—from his head. "That would be great. First thing to research is that 'no bail' issue. My guess is Welles is full of shit. That provision has been in the Constitution since 1889. I bet there's case law that interprets it the way we want."

"That's why he did it orally," Yamata suggested. "If it was written, you would have had time to research it."

Brunelle grimaced. "Yeah, he's pretty sleazy. But it might come back to bite him if Quinn feels like he tricked her."

"Is there anything else we need?" Yamata asked.

Brunelle rubbed his chin. "It might be useful to know whether we can rely on Holly's statement even if we don't have her on board. Once Jess gets wind of our predicament, she's gonna squeeze me—*us*—for a better deal."

Yamata stood up and leaned over his desk. He managed not to look at her chest. Just barely. "My briefs will be on your desk in the morning."

Brunelle sighed. "Great, Michelle. Great."

CHAPTER 9

"Dismissal?" Brunelle was incredulous. "Is that supposed to be a joke?"

"No joke, Dave." Edwards leaned back in the chair across Brunelle's desk. She had stopped by after court on another matter. Nothing like face-to-face negotiations. "I heard what happened this morning. The whole courthouse is talking about it. Welles kicked your ass."

"Welles' client is in on ten million dollars bail," replied Brunelle. "That's not exactly an ass-kicking."

"He should be in on no bail," observed Edwards.

"He will be."

"Not without my client." Edwards crossed her arms and grinned. "Dismissal."

Brunelle appreciated the hardball tactics, but he wasn't about to dismiss one case outright to maybe get a conviction on another.

"Well, here's what I know." Brunelle folded his hands on his desk. "I have two defendants. One of them gave a full confession. So I'm going to get at least one conviction. It's up to you and your client to decide whether it will be her or him."

Edwards' smile faded just a bit. Just enough for Brunelle to know she understood.

"Don't get me wrong, Jess. I would much rather convict Arpad Karpati. I believe Holly when she says it was all his idea and he did it while she puked in the bathroom. But Welles has a point. It's a very self-serving statement. She really minimizes. I cut her a dismissal and the jury may well believe I jumped to conclusions and cut the wrong person a deal. But if she pleads to something less, like maybe burglary, she'll do less than a year in juvi prison, and when I put her on the stand, that very conviction supports one of the aggravators I'll be trying to prove. Fits nicely with my case theory."

"Case theory?" Edwards laughed bitterly. "Listen to you. I'm talking about a young girl's life and you're worrying about your case theory."

Brunelle raised an eyebrow. "It's not like her hands are totally clean in this, Jess. She knew exactly what that bastard was gonna do, and she still knocked on that girl's door."

Edwards didn't have a response ready for that.

"Don't try to hardball me, Jess. I'll cut her a fair deal, but I'm not desperate. Michelle Yamata is already working on the brief that'll get Karpati in on a no-bail hold, regardless of whether Holly is smart enough to save her skin."

"Michelle Yamata?" Jess practically choked. "Yamata's your second chair?" She started to laugh. "That cheerleader's gonna file a sexual harassment claim on you the second the case is over."

Brunelle forced a smile. "You think she'll wait that long?" he joked darkly.

"Well, of course, Dave. She'll want to notch a capital case in her belt before she gets your ass fired."

Brunelle nodded. "Great."

"All right, no dismissal," Jess changed the subject back to their negotiations. "But I don't like burglary. How about rendering criminal assistance? Burglary is a level eight offense. With her history that means mandatory time in juvi. You cut her a rendering and at least I can argue for credit for time served and probation."

Brunelle pursed his lips. He drummed his fingers on his desk. He pushed himself back into his chair.

"I have to think about it, Jess. That's a huge reduction. From aggravated murder one all the way down to rendering criminal assistance? I'll have a lot of explaining to do."

That reminded him. Brunelle slapped the desk. "Damn it. I gotta talk to the family before I can offer anything. I almost forgot."

"What if they say no?" Jess furrowed her brow. "You're not going to let them have the final say, are you?"

"Of course not," replied Brunelle. "They don't have any say. It's my call. But they need to think they had a say. I have to at least pretend to listen to them, explain the options, and tell them why they should agree with what I'm going to do anyway."

Edwards looked at her watch. "Well, you better hurry, Dave. That bail hearing is gonna be here before you know it."

Brunelle nodded. "Yeah, I know. And I have to meet with someone else first."

CHAPTER 10

"Grande triple americano with one ice cube, please," Kat told the barista.

"One ice cube?" Brunelle asked as he pulled out his wallet.

"I like to drink it fast," explained Kat. "And put your wallet away. At least for my drink. I'm paying for myself."

Brunelle smiled. "Okay. As long as you're not paying for me too. I don't want to owe you anything."

Kat looked him up and down. Then she started laughing. "Like hell you don't."

She took her drink and headed for a small table in the corner. Brunelle ordered a brewed coffee and in a few minutes joined her.

"As much as I'd like to think the coffee invite was because of my dazzling eyes," Kat batted her eyelashes over her drink, "this is business, isn't it?"

Brunelle shrugged and took a sip from his still too-hot coffee. "Probably both. But yeah, I do need to talk to you about the

Montgomery case. Have you done the autopsy yet?"

"Are you kidding? That was a week ago. We don't let them back up like that. I've done that and a dozen more since."

Brunelle smiled tightly. "Wonderful."

Kat laughed again. "I love my job."

"That's great. Really. I couldn't do it, I know that."

"It's almost like opening Christmas presents," Kat enthused. "You never know what you're going to find inside."

"Wow," laughed Brunelle. "Remind me not to let you join our secret Santa this year."

Kat shook her head. "Fine, Mr. Squeamish. What do you want to know about the Montgomery autopsy?"

Brunelle was bothered that she might think less of him for being squeamish, but he decided not to protest. He was a lawyer, not a pathologist. He'd never keep up with her on that front.

"Maybe," Brunelle tried, "it might be best if I just lay it all out on the table."

Kat laughed. "That's generally how I work."

Brunelle smiled and shook his head.

"Sorry," said Kat. "Couldn't resist. By all means, overwhelm me with honesty and candor."

Brunelle sipped again, then got right to it. "I have two defendants. One confessed, but basically implicated the other. And the other lawyered up."

"Yeah, I already knew all that."

Brunelle screwed up his face. "You did?"

"Well, I read the paper. And besides," she took a long drink of her coffee, "everybody's talking about how Welles kicked your ass in court."

"He did not kick my ass!"

The other patrons turned to look at Brunelle. He started to

blush. Kat burst out laughing.

"Oh, you are fun, David Brunelle."

"He did not kick my ass," Brunelle repeated in a lower voice. "I still got ten mil on his client. But yes, his client is the one who lawyered up. The girl wants a dismissal, and I want to know if there's anything forensically that supports the fact that Welles' client was the killer."

Kat's radiant smile finally faded as she pursed her lips in thought. But her eyes still sparkled and Brunelle wondered if she could tell just how glad he was to be with her right then, no matter how grisly the conversation.

"We did fingernail clippings," Kat considered. "DNA might have linked him, but the crime lab said the only profile was hers."

"Anything from the autopsy to support a larger person, a man, versus, say, a fifteen year old girl?"

Kat gave a noncommittal shrug. "Maybe. The bindings on the wrists were tight, the flesh was pressed in very deep. That suggests strength. Then there's the whole issue of pulling a hundred-pound body up off the ground and tying it off on the balcony."

"She was only one hundred pounds?"

"Yeah she was a small little thing."

That reminded him of something else he needed to ask. Something that would corroborate, to a degree anyway, Holly's claims. But he wasn't entirely sure how to ask it.

"Um. How thorough are your autopsies?"

Kat cocked her head. "Very thorough. Of course. That's the whole point."

Brunelle nodded. "Right, right." He took a nervous sip of his coffee. "Look, I need to ask a question, and it's fine if you don't know the answer. I don't imagine it's something you check usually.

But I just want you to know there's a reason I'm asking and please don't shout out the question back to me in this crowded, already suspicious of me coffee house."

Kat listened intently, then laughed again. Brunelle really liked how her mouth looked when she laughed. "Okay, David. Wow. I promise. Now you've got me curious. What piece of information do you want to know from my examination of a dead thirteen year old girl's body?"

Brunelle took a bracing sip of his coffee. "Was she a virgin?"

Kat pursed her lips and took another long drag from her coffee. "Please tell me you're not a pervert."

Before Brunelle could respond, Kat added, "Well, at least not that kind of pervert."

Brunelle was pretty sure he blushed, although he wasn't exactly sure whether it was because of what he had asked or what she had suggested. "No, not that kind of pervert."

He explained what Holly had said about Karpati needing a virgin for a victim.

"Are you fucking kidding me?" Kat said. "He thinks he's a vampire?"

Brunelle shrugged. "That's what the girl said."

"Does he sparkle?" Kat laughed.

"No, he's old school. Transylvanian royalty and all that."

Kat drank again. "Well, Mr. Pervert. I guess I can help after all. Yes, she was a virgin. We checked for evidence of sexual assault. There were no signs of trauma, and her hymen was in tact."

Brunelle nodded and sipped at his coffee.

"Happy now?" Kat asked.

Brunelle frowned. "Not really. She's still dead."

Kat's usual smile faded a bit. "She was dead before you got involved, David. You can't change that. You can just try to bring her and her family some justice."

Brunelle nodded and managed a faint grin. "Thanks, Kat."

He looked at his watch. "I better get back to the office."

"Aww," pouted Kat. "I haven't finished my coffee."

Then she tipped her head back and downed the rest of her drink all at once. "Okay, that's better. Thanks for the date, David."

They both stood up. "We'll have to do this again sometime," Brunelle said casually.

"Great," Kat slipped an arm through his. "When?"

Brunelle was taken aback. But he was used to thinking on his feet. And taking advantage of a beneficial statement.

"How's next Friday?" suggested Brunelle. "Dinner maybe. I'll even let you buy."

Kat laughed as they stepped out of the door. "Oh, how kind of you. But you'd owe me."

"Right. That was the plan."

Then Kat slapped her forehead. "Wait, next Friday? No I can't. My daughter has a recital that night."

"Ahh," said Brunelle, but what he meant was 'Ohh, you have kids.'

"Yes, I am divorced and I have a daughter, Mr. Brunelle," Kat replied. "A wonderful fourteen-year-old daughter named Lizzy, who has a ballet recital next Friday night. Is that gonna be a problem?"

"Not for me," Brunelle answered. "But she's probably gonna be upset that you're missing her recital."

Kat laughed. "How about the Friday after that? She'll be visiting her dad in Portland that weekend."

"Oh yeah?" Brunelle asked.

"Oh, yeah," purred Kat.

Brunelle smiled. "It's a date."

CHAPTER 11

Yamata's briefs were, in fact, exquisite.

Welles was a lying sack of crap. Brunelle knew it, but Yamata reduced it to writing.

"Very nice," Brunelle said to her over the pleadings as he finished. "Let's get these filed today."

He looked at the last page. It was prepared for his signature. "One change though. Make these for your signature."

"Oh," said Yamata. "I just figured, since you're lead..."

"I'm co," corrected Brunelle. "And you wrote them, so you get to sign them."

Yamata shifted in her seat.

"You're not at a private firm anymore, Michelle. And I'm not some partner looking for an ego massage."

He immediately regretted the 'massage' reference, but figured she knew what he meant.

"That's nice to know, Mr. Bru—, er, Dave. But there's

something else. What if they're no good."

Brunelle smiled. "No worries there. They're great. In fact," he leaned forward, "why don't you argue it?"

Yamata choked. "Me? You're lead."

"Co. And yes, you. You wrote the briefs. You know it better than I do. It'll lose something in the translation."

"Uh, okay. Great. Thanks, Mr. Br—, uh, Dave."

"Now," Brunelle stood up. "Ready to meet the parents?"

Yamata stood up too and put a hand to her stomach. "Ugh. Wow, really? No. I'm not sure I could ever be ready for that."

Brunelle smiled. "That's exactly the right answer. Now come on, this time you can let me do the talking."

Yamata exhaled loudly. "Yes, sir. Thank you, sir. May I have another?"

Brunelle glanced at her. She smiled and curtsied.

"Glad you're enjoying yourself," Brunelle laughed. "Because this next part is going to suck."

***

Mr. and Mrs. Montgomery were already in the conference room, along with Tammy Gardner of the victims and witnesses support division. Mr. Montgomery stood up as Brunelle and Yamata walked in. Mrs. Montgomery remained seated next to Tammy, who patted her shoulder supportively.

"Mr. Brunelle." Montgomery stuck out his hand. "Good to see you again. Tammy told us you filed the death notice. Thank you."

Despite Brunelle's job, it still seemed like a strange thing to thank someone for. But he had stopped a long time ago trying to understand or anticipate the emotions of murder victim families.

"It's well warranted," Brunelle answered as he shook Montgomery's hand. "Let me introduce Michelle Yamata, the other prosecutor on the case."

Yamata extended her hand too, but Mr. Montgomery ignored it. "You need two prosecutors? Why? Is there a problem with the case?"

"Roger! Please." Mrs. Montgomery huffed at him but he ignored her.

It was like they were all still out by the patrol car the night of the murder. Brunelle managed not to roll his eyes.

"Just the opposite, Mr. Montgomery," Brunelle answered. "We always put two attorneys on a death case. And Michelle is one of our best attorneys."

Mr. Montgomery looked her up and down. "Yes. Well. I can see that."

And then everyone was uncomfortable.

"Why don't we have a seat, Mr. Montgomery?" Yamata motioned to the chairs surrounding the table. "Mr. Brunelle and I have some things to tell you and we'd like to hear your input."

Brunelle was impressed by how Yamata grabbed control of the situation. Montgomery stopped leering and sat next to his wife, who whispered at him to be quiet and listen.

"I'm sure Tammy has already let you know that we've charged two people with the murder of your daughter," Brunelle started. "One adult and one juvenile."

"And you're seeking death on both, right?" Mr. Montgomery wanted to confirm.

Brunelle shook his head. "I'm afraid not. Juveniles can never be executed. The U.S. Supreme Court has held it to be unconstitutional."

"What, never?"

"No, never," confirmed Brunelle. "But that may be just as well."

Mr. Montgomery was about to argue, when Mrs. Montgomery stepped in. "How do you mean, Mr. Brunelle?"

"Well, we have some important decisions moving forward as we try to bring your daughter's killer or killers to justice. Unfortunately, the entire system is stacked against us. A defendant is presumed innocent. We don't just have to prove the case, we have to prove it beyond a reasonable doubt. If a suspect refuses to talk and asks for a lawyer, we can't tell that to the jury. We have to give them every last police report, every last sticky note any cop or any other witness ever creates about the case. They don't have to give us anything. And the jury will be told again and again by the judge that if they aren't sure about something, then they have to give the defendant the benefit of any doubt."

"Sounds like you think you can't win the case," sniffed Mr. Montgomery.

"Hush, Roger. It sounds like he's being honest." Mrs. Montgomery turned back to Brunelle. "So what do you have planned?"

"Well, this isn't about a plan," Brunelle said. "I just want to explain to you where we're at and what we're facing."

"All right then, Mr. Brunelle," said Mrs. Montgomery. "Where are we at, and what are we facing?"

Brunelle took a deep breath. "There are two people responsible for your daughter's murder," he explained. "A twenty-year-old man and a fifteen-year-old girl. The twenty-year-old man is the major player. It was his idea, he recruited the girl to help, and he did the actual deed.

"The girl is the minor player. She was just along for the ride, and was actually a victim of the man too. She was underage, but he forced himself on her sexually. So we have a pretty clear cut, evil bad guy, and a pretty clear cut, less culpable juvenile who was used by this guy."

Neither Montgomery said anything, but they were both leaning forward, ready for more.

"The girl isn't looking at much punishment anyway," Brunelle continued. "She's a juvenile. We can't seek the death penalty, and if she stays in the juvenile system, which is a better than fifty-fifty chance, she'll only do a few years."

"That's bullshit," said Mr. Montgomery.

"You're absolutely right," answered Brunelle. "But it's the reality of the situation. Here's another reality. We don't have any evidence against the twenty-year-old man. He's gonna walk."

"What?" cried Mrs. Montgomery. "The man responsible for murdering Emily is going to get away with it? How can you say that?"

"I can't convict him without evidence," Brunelle shrugged. "But he lawyered up. That is, he asked for an attorney and refused to give a statement. The only witness I have is the girl, but I can't call her as a witness because she's a defendant herself. She has the right to remain silent. Which is too bad, because she gave a full confession which totally and completely implicated the man."

"Can't you just play the confession then?" Mr. Montgomery asked.

Brunelle frowned and shook his head. "I'm afraid not. The man—Karpati is his name—Karpati has the constitutional right to confront and question his accusers. We can't play a tape from the girl without putting the girl on the stand for his lawyer to cross examine. But like I said, we can't put her on the stand because she has the right to remain silent."

Mr. Montgomery's face started to turn a blotchy red, and his clenched fists were shaking. Mrs. Montgomery's eyes were starting to glisten.

"So as it stands now," Brunelle concluded, "if nothing changes, I expect to convict the girl in juvenile court and get a few years on her. And I expect the man to be acquitted, if a judge doesn't throw the case out before that."

"That's not very good news, Mr. Brunelle," said Mrs. Montgomery. "I'm not sure what I expected but it wasn't that."

Mr. Montgomery stood up and gazed out the window. Brunelle looked at Yamata. Her eyes were wide and she sported a deep frown. He nodded ever so slightly to her.

"You know... There is one thing we could do," she said. "But we would never do it without your permission."

"What is it?" Mr. Montgomery spun from the window.

Yamata looked to Brunelle to explain. He was nodding and tapping his lips. "Well, like I said, the girl isn't facing much anyway. If we cut her some kind of deal. Some sort of reduction. Nothing too big. But on the condition she testify. Well, I suppose, we wouldn't lose all that much on her, since she wasn't facing much anyway. But then we'd have the best damn witness we could against the twenty-year-old."

The Montgomerys just stared at him.

"If we did that, we could get him." Then Brunelle drove the point home, "And we can kill him."

"Do it," said Mr. Montgomery. "Do whatever you have to do in order to hold that bastard fully responsible for Emily's murder."

Brunelle looked at the mother. "Mrs. Montgomery?"

She stared down for several moments. Then her shoulders dropped and she looked away. "Yes. Do it. Do whatever you have to do."

CHAPTER 12

"All rise!" The judicial assistant banged the gavel as Judge Caruthers took the bench. "The King County Superior Court, Juvenile Division is now in session."

The judge nodded and Brunelle and Yamata took their seats at the prosecutor's table. Edwards sat opposite them at the defense table.

"Are the parties ready on the matter of the State of Washington versus Holly Sandholm?" the judge asked even as he fiddled with the computer monitor on the bench.

"Yes, Your Honor," Brunelle answered.

"I believe so," Edwards responded.

"And this is a plea to amended charges, is that right?" asked the judge.

"Yes, Your Honor," Brunelle stood up to explain. "The State is amending the charges to residential burglary, in exchange for which, Ms. Sandholm is agreeing to plead guilty to the amended charge."

"Have you gone over the guilty plea form with your client, Ms. Edwards?" Judge Caruthers asked.

"I have, Your Honor," Edwards answered. "I am confident she understands it."

The judge looked over to the guards. "Bring in Ms. Sandholm."

The guards unlocked the door and yelled, "Sandholm!" into the holding area. After a moment, Holly stepped through the door and sat down next to her lawyer.

Brunelle was struck by how much better she looked than that day in the interview room. She had put on at least five pounds and was clean. Even in the jail jammies, she was definitely in better shape than on the outside.

Brunelle saw Sandholm whisper something into Edwards' ear and noticed Edwards' eyebrows shoot up.

Edwards raised a hand toward the bench. "Uh, may I have a moment to speak with my client, Your Honor?"

"Of course, counsel," Judge Caruthers replied without looking away from his computer, his mouse clicking periodically. The rumor in the courthouse was he played solitaire all day while just ratifying whatever the attorneys had agreed to. Not that that was necessarily a bad thing. Sometimes it's good to know a judge won't go sideways on a plea bargain. But Brunelle wasn't worried about the judge going sideways.

"Is there a problem, Jess?" he whispered to Edwards. Mr. and Mrs. Montgomery were in the gallery behind him.

Edwards didn't reply audibly, but waved him away while she was whispering with Holly.

Brunelle looked at Yamata and shrugged. She shrugged back. They waited, Brunelle's anxiety rising with each second.

Finally, Edwards nodded at Holly, then stood up to address the judge.

"My client has changed her mind, Your Honor," she announced. "She does not want to plead guilty."

Brunelle heard the outraged "What?" from Mr. Montgomery behind him. Mrs. Montgomery said something too, but he couldn't quite make it out. It wasn't anything good though, he knew. Brunelle stood up as well. "May I have a moment to speak to counsel, Your Honor?"

"Of course," replied the judge. Brunelle wondered if he'd gotten all the aces yet.

"What the hell's going on, Jess?" he whispered to his counterpart.

"She changed her mind, Dave," Edwards whispered back. "She doesn't want to plead."

Brunelle clenched his jaw. "Is she holding out for the rendering criminal assistance charge? You told me she'd plead to burglary."

"No, she's not holding out. I specifically asked her that, and she said she wouldn't plead to anything."

Brunelle tapped his hand on his leg. "Tell her I'll give her the damn rendering, Jess. I need her to plead."

"I know, but she doesn't want it. I'm telling you. Something changed since I talked to her yesterday. She was totally on board with the burglary and testifying. Now all she'll say is 'I'm not pleading and I'm not testifying.'"

"Counsel?" the judge finally turned from his computer. Must have run out of moves. "Where are we?"

"We need to strike the plea," Edwards answered.

Brunelle narrowed his eyes. "And schedule a motion to transfer the case to adult court."

"Come on, Dave," Edwards whispered. "Give me a chance to work on her."

"Fuck her, Jess," Brunelle whispered back. "She doesn't want to testify against him, then she can sit next to him. I may not be able to have her executed, but she can spend the next three decades in prison."

***

"What the hell was that?" Brunelle demanded of Edwards once they were in the conference room between the courtroom and the hallway. The hallway where he knew the Montgomerys were waiting to yell at him.

Edwards shrugged. "I told you. She doesn't want any deals any more. She said she doesn't even care if the case is transferred to adult court."

"Did you tell her she'll die in prison?"

"Oh yeah, she gets that."

"Well, good," Yamata chimed in. "She deserves it anyway for what she did."

Brunelle winced. This was about negotiations and trying to get to the best possible result. It was also about long term professional relationships with defense attorneys you see again and again and again. It might also be about someone getting what they deserve, but you don't say that out loud. Not to Jessica Edwards anyway.

"What she deserves?" Edwards snapped. "A fifteen year-old-girl who was raped and controlled by a twenty-year-old man doesn't deserve to spend her entire life in prison."

"A fifteen-year-old girl," Yamata shot back, "who knocked on Emily Montgomery's door knowing what that twenty-year-old man was gonna do to her? Who staked out the place and waited for her parents to leave? Who made the entire damn thing possible?

Who didn't come forward until she was arrested and even then hesitated to tell the truth? Yeah, she deserves to die in prison. She deserves worse."

Edwards' face was turning red. But before she could respond, Yamata finished with, "Tell me what Emily Montgomery deserved?"

Edwards glared at Brunelle, who just offered a pained smile and a shrug.

"You just lost any chance at a deal, Dave," Edwards hissed. "See you at the transfer hearing."

Edwards stormed out of the conference room, slamming the door behind her.

"What a bitch," Yamata growled.

Brunelle shook his head. "Naw, Jessica's all right. She's just a true believer."

Yamata cocked her head. "A what?"

"Jess thinks everybody is basically good and sometimes people make mistakes. She thinks cops lie and prosecutors only care about winning. Every one of her clients is being treated unfairly and it's her job to protect them from the powerful government that's trying to put them away for something they didn't really do."

Yamata's jaw dropped. "Does she really believe that?"

"I think so," Brunelle nodded. "Being a criminal defense attorney is a tough job. Defending people who've committed crimes takes a special mindset. A lot of people can't look themselves in the mirror. It's worse if you're a public defender. If you're a private attorney and some psychopath comes into your office, you can always say no. But Edwards gets a file on her desk and she has to represent that psychopath. And worse yet, the psychopath thinks she sucks because she's a 'public pretender,' even though she's probably tried twice as many cases as your typical private defense attorney."

Brunelle smiled as Yamata processed the information.

"Just don't bring up the victim," Brunelle smiled. "She hates being reminded there's a victim."

"But that's the whole point of criminal law," Yamata argued, "to vindicate the victim."

"Maybe," Brunelle shrugged. "But you have to know when to bring it up with her. It tends to piss her off."

Yamata crossed her arms. "I can see that."

"So bring it up just before her closing argument," Brunelle winked. "Totally fucks with her."

Yamata laughed out loud. "Oh, Mr. Brunelle, I like that."

Brunelle smirked. "I thought you might. And remember, it's Dave."

"Right. Dave." She saluted and offered a fabulous smile. "Don't want you to feel old when you're around me."

Brunelle wasn't sure what to say, so he changed the subject. "Come on, let's go get yelled at by the parents."

***

"What just happened?" Mr. Montgomery demanded as soon as they stepped into the hallway.

"Change in plans," Brunelle smiled. "But nothing we can't deal with."

"I thought you said you needed her?" Mrs. Montgomery pointed out.

"I did," Brunelle conceded, "but part of my job—part of our job," he gestured to Yamata, "is to be prepared for any contingency and move forward with the prosecution."

"Can you do that?" Mr. Montgomery questioned.

"Definitely," Brunelle asserted, although he wasn't really sure how. Then he realized something. "Although not the rape of a child count. That will have to be dismissed without Holly's testimony."

Mr. Montgomery shrugged. "Well, it hardly matters if he gets a death sentence. The jury will still hear about the sick pervert, right?"

Brunelle shook his head. "I'm afraid not. Too prejudicial."

"But it's the truth," Mrs. Montgomery protested.

"I wish this were about the truth," Yamata said, "but it's about evidence. If we get too close to the child rape allegation, it could result in a mistrial."

"Followed by a motion to dismiss," Brunelle agreed, "for governmental misconduct. We'll paint the picture. The jury should be able to connect the dots."

Mr. Montgomery looked at his wife, then back at the attorneys. "Well, I don't really give a damn right now about what happened to Holly What's-her-name. I care what happened to Emily. You're sure the murder prosecution can go forward without her?"

"I'm sure," Brunelle lied.

"Then that's good enough for us," Mr. Montgomery announced.

"I do have a question," Mrs. Montgomery said. "Do you know why she changed her mind?"

"I don't *know*," Brunelle answered, "but I have a guess."

"What's your guess?"

"Karpati."

CHAPTER 13

Brunelle and Yamata retreated to Brunelle's office to regroup.

"Now what?" Yamata asked, dropping her athletic frame into one of his guest chairs.

Brunelle picked up the phone. "Now we order Holly's jail calls. Somebody got to her."

"How can you be so sure?"

"Because this is suicide," Brunelle answered as he punched the extension for the jail communications officer. "She gave a full confession to a heinous murder. No way she doesn't get convicted. And no way she doesn't get life. It's mandatory."

"Any chance she doesn't get transferred to adult court," Yamata asked, "since the penalty is so severe?"

Brunelle frowned. That was a good point. Luckily the jail officer picked up. "Yeah, this is Dave Brunelle from the prosecutor's office. I need to order some jail recordings."

When Brunelle hung up, he had ordered all calls coming into Holly's dorm and all calls going out of Karpati's holding tank. They were supposed to have individual caller identification codes, but inmates were always using somebody else's code to try to be sneaky. It still amazed Brunelle how freely people would talk even after hearing the automated 'This call will be recorded' warning.

"It'll take them a couple days to get us the recordings," Brunelle informed his co-counsel, "but we should have them before the transfer hearing."

"What about tomorrow's bail hearing?" Yamata asked. "We won't be able to tell the judge that Holly's on board to testify."

Brunelle smiled. "Then I hope you do a good job arguing that brief you wrote."

Yamata slumped back in her chair. "Great."

Brunelle's phone rang and he picked it up without even looking at the caller I.D. "Prosecutor's office. Dave Brunelle."

"Hello, prosecutor's-office-Dave-Brunelle," sang the voice on the phone. "This is medical-examiner's-office-Kat-Anderson. Can you talk?"

Brunelle smiled. "For you? Of course."

Yamata leaned forward. "Do you want me to leave?" she whispered.

Brunelle shook his head. He figured it was business. He was wrong.

"So about Friday night," Kat went on, "I have an idea."

Brunelle drew a blank, still in work mode. "Friday night?"

"My daughter's recital, remember?"

"Ah yes. Right. Recital." Brunelle laughed. "I was trying to forget the pain from you turning down my asking you out for that night."

Yamata stood up. "I'm gonna go now," she whispered

again.

This time Brunelle nodded. "I'll stop by later," he whispered over the covered-up telephone receiver. "We can figure out how to tackle tomorrow."

"Is this a bad time?" Kat asked.

"Hmm? Oh, no. Never a bad time for you, ma'am."

"Ma'am?" Kat laughed. "You're way older than me."

Brunelle frowned. "I am not *way* older than you."

"I didn't say too old," Kat purred.

Brunelle could feel himself blush a little, and was glad Yamata had excused herself.

"So I have a solution," Kat went on.

"To what?" Brunelle wondered if she was back talking about the case.

"To you being crushed by my remorseless rejection of you."

"Great," Brunelle chuckled. "I'm all for not being remorselessly rejected."

"Good," said Kat. "The recital starts at seven. Meet me in the lobby at quarter till."

"Uhhh," Brunelle stammered. "Recital? Your daughter's ballet recital?"

"No, my dog's violin recital," Kat huffed. "Of course. It's at the Roosevelt High School performing arts center on sixty-fifth. I have to drop her off by six-thirty, so I'll meet you in the lobby at six-forty-five."

Brunelle hesitated, then was smart enough to say, "Uh, okay. Sounds great. Uh, what should I wear?"

"Just come straight from work," Kat said. "Wear your suit. Lizzy will be impressed."

"Your daughter?"

"You are on top of it today, David," Kat teased. "Yes. And if she likes you, maybe you can get ice cream with us afterwards."

"Ballet and ice cream," Brunelle repeated. "Two of my favorite things."

Kat laughed. "You are so full of it."

Brunelle laughed too. "Well, I like ice cream."

CHAPTER 14

"I understand you were unable to secure the cooperation of Miss Sandholm." Welles' smirk to his seated and handcuffed client confirmed for Brunelle that Karpati was responsible for convincing the girl not to turn State's evidence.

Brunelle smiled. "I just wanted your guy to have some company during the trial."

"I can't imagine you could try them together," Welles replied, "since you've charged him with raping her."

"Imagine me dumping that charge," Brunelle replied just as Judge Quinn took the bench,

"All rise!"

Judge Quinn instructed everyone to be seated and asked whether the parties were ready for the bail hearing.

"Absolutely, Your Honor," gushed Welles.

Brunelle didn't say anything. He looked to Yamata seated next to him. She didn't say anything either, so he nudged her.

"Uh, y— yes, Your Honor," Yamata stood up. "The State is ready."

Judge Quinn raised her eyebrow. "Will you be arguing this, Miss...?"

"Yamata. Michelle Yamata. And yes, I wrote the brief, and I'll be arguing it."

Brunelle heard Welles chuckle and saw him whisper something to his client. Karpati smiled as he leered at Yamata.

"Very well," Judge Quinn said. "Let's start with the State then. Tell me what you want me to do, and why I should do it."

"May I interrupt?" Wells shot to his feet. "I believe there is some additional information of which the court ought to be informed before the State begins its argument."

Yamata scowled at him, but waited for the judge to say who could speak.

"What is it, Mr. Welles?"

"As you undoubtedly recall, Your Honor," Welles rolled a hand for emphasis, "the State placed great reliance on their ability to persuade a young lady, whom they have charged with this murder, to agree to testify against my client. It is my understanding that this girl has declined offers to so testify, and therefore the representations made at the previous hearing by Mr. Brunelle were demonstrably false. I would ask the court not only to refuse to hear any motion for reconsideration of bail, but further to sanction Mr. Brunelle and the prosecutor's office for misleading the tribunal and wasting my time. My fees and costs for being here today total over one thousand dollars. That is the minimum the court should impose on the prosecution. Thank you."

Yamata's eyes bulged wide and she looked down at Brunelle, who was still seated at counsel table. Brunelle let out an irritated exhale and stood up. "May I be heard on this, Your

Honor?"

"Of course, Mr. Brunelle," the judge replied. "But first, tell me this: Is that girl going to testify or not?"

"Not," he answered.

"We repeat our motion for sanctions, Your Honor," Welles piped in.

"Be quiet, Mr. Welles," said Judge Quinn calmly. Then, turning back to Brunelle, "Why did you tell me that she would testify against Mr. Karpati?"

"Because I honestly thought that she would," Brunelle answered. "In fact we had a plea hearing set yesterday and everyone, including her lawyer, expected her to accept the State's offer. However, at the last moment, she refused to plead guilty."

Judge Quinn nodded. "Do you know why she changed her mind."

Brunelle surrendered a sardonic smile. "Not yet, Your Honor." He glanced at Karpati. "But we're looking into it."

Welles jumped out of his chair. "This is outrageous, Your Honor! First, Mr. Brunelle intentionally lied to the court. Now, he casts aspersions against my client and myself! I have never—"

"You can stop now, Mr. Welles," Judge Quinn interrupted. "He told me he had a good faith belief the girl would testify. I don't think Mr. Brunelle was lying. He ended up being mistaken, but that happens a lot in this line of work."

She turned back to Brunelle. "So should we just strike this hearing then, since you won't be able to show clear evidence of the crime to justify a no bail hold?"

"No, Your Honor," Yamata answered. "The hearing should go forward."

Judge Quinn looked back at Brunelle's junior partner. "And why is that, Miss...?"

"Yamata," she said with only a hint of irritation at having to say it again so soon. "And the reason why is that Mr. Welles' legal argument to the court was mistaken at best, misleading at worse, and in any event incorrect."

Welles turned red in the face. Brunelle—and Judge Quinn— suppressed a smile. Yamata kept her poker face, staring straight at the judge.

"I have filed a brief explaining all that, Your Honor," Yamata continued. "We did not receive any response brief from Mr. Welles."

Brunelle looked over and saw Karpati's eyebrows knit together as his mouth curled into a scowl. He could see why Holly might be afraid of him. He smacked Welles' arm and the defense attorney leaned down for Karpati to whisper something in his ear. The two exchanged heated whispers for a few moments. Then Welles stood up straight again. "My client has instructed me to file a response brief. I did not think it necessary given the misdeeds of the prosecution."

"Our brief was served on them in a timely fashion," Yamata protested. "We're ready to argue this today."

Judge Quinn raised her hand. "Counsel, counsel. Let's all step back from the precipice."

She turned to Welles. "How much time do you need, counsel?"

"One week, Your Honor. No more."

"Ms Yamata, will the State be ready to argue the motion in one week?"

"We're ready to argue it now."

Judge Quinn smiled, but Brunelle could see her patience was wearing thin. "So we'll be ready in a week as well, Your Honor," he interjected.

Judge Quinn smiled. "All right then. Here is what we're going to do. We will reschedule the bail hearing for one week from today. We will also schedule a pre-trial conference to discuss any other matters that might need to be discussed."

"May I suggest a continuance motion as well, Your Honor?" Brunelle spoke up. "I can speak with counsel in the meantime about possible dates for trial. I'm thinking probably the spring, Mr. Welles?"

Welles didn't look back at Brunelle. "We will object to any continuance. We demand a speedy trial."

The speedy trial rule in Washington required the trial to start within ninety days of the arraignment, unless the defendant was in custody, in which case it had to start within sixty days. They'd already lost seven days on the bail issue. Murder cases were always continued out past the sixty-day deadline upon agreement of the parties. Hell, joy riding cases were routinely continued out past the sixty-day rule.

Judge Quinn raised an eyebrow. "You're going to be ready to start a capital murder case in fifty-three days, Mr. Welles?"

"I will Your Honor."

Brunelle was getting tired of Welles' bravado.

"At least I will be more prepared than the State," Welles went on. "I see defense attorneys routinely agree to continuances so that the State can get its DNA results back from the lab, or something equally damaging to the accused. I will not agree to give the State more time to manufacture evidence against my wholly innocent client."

Brunelle had to smile. The man had a point. He never did understand why defense attorneys would give him more time. Well, he did understand. They weren't ready either. But it was more than that. They weren't assholes like Welles.

"Fine, Your Honor," Brunelle addressed the court. "The State can be ready within the speedy trial expiration. But I would ask that the court make a finding that the defense has answered ready for trial. I don't think they should be allowed to challenge us to be ready, and then when we are ready, they ask for a continuance and claim to need more time to prepare."

Quinn looked back at Welles. "The man has a point. You want a speedy trial, I'll give you a speedy trial. But I'm not going to let you out of it, if turns out you guessed wrong and they really can get ready that fast."

Welles smiled, but Brunelle could see the worry hidden in the corners of his mouth. "We'll be ready, Your Honor. And my client will be acquitted."

Judge Quinn wisely didn't comment. Instead, she announced the schedule. "Trial will be scheduled for six weeks from today. We will have a status conference two weeks before trial. In one week from today we will have a preliminary pre-trial conference. In addition we will have a bail hearing. In the meantime, I am changing Mr. Karpati's conditions of release to a no bail hold."

"What?" Welles shouted. "We haven't had the bail hearing!"

"You're correct, Mr. Welles," the judge responded, "because you weren't ready. But I've read Ms. Yamata's brief and I think she's probably right. I'm not going to give your client a chance to post bail while we wait for a full hearing. No bail hold. Court is adjourned."

Judge Quinn stood up and retreated to her chambers.

Brunelle was going to say something smarmy to Welles, but Karpati was already grabbing at Welles' shirt sleeve.

Yamata stepped next to Brunelle and purred, "Told ya my briefs were exquisite."

CHAPTER 15

The recital was at seven. Brunelle was supposed to be there at six forty-five. It was maybe twenty minutes from his office. But he didn't really feel like working past six that night. In fact, he didn't feel like working past five.

So he decided to take the long way to the high school. Actually, the totally opposite way, then double back. If he was going to try to convict Karpati without Holly, he was going to need to find someone else. There may not have been anyone else with the two of them that night, but people talk. And anything you say can and will be used against you. People think that just applies to things you say to the cops. Brunelle knew better. He hoped Karpati didn't.

He parked his car right in front of 'Darkness.'

It was early still, for a nightclub anyway, but he thought they might be open already. And he kind of wanted to miss most of the clientele. If anybody was going to know what Arpad Karpati was really about, it was going to be the staff. Maybe the regulars, but Brunelle wasn't sure he was ready to meet the regulars quite yet. He buttoned his suit coat, smoothed back his just-starting-to-gray hair, and pulled open the faux castle door.

He had been kind of looking forward to the record-scratching, piano-stopping, everybody-looking-at-the-door reaction his suited entry into the underground nightclub would evoke. He was disappointed.

There were three other guys in suits drinking beers in the corner, and the bartender, a young woman covered in black clothes, silver jewelry, and colorful tattoos, looked up and said, not at all ominously, "Hi."

"Uh, hi," Brunelle answered. He walked over to the bar. "Can I get a beer?"

He wasn't going to do more than sip at it while he talked to the bartender. Not right before driving across town. He didn't think there would—or should—be a lot of tolerance for a prosecutor drinking and driving.

The bartender slid him a bottle of the latest local microbrew and was about to turn away.

"Thanks, uh, what did you say your name was?"

The woman stopped and stared at him. An 'are-you-fucking-kidding-me' kind of stare.

"Seriously, mister," she said. "You're old enough to be my dad. Which means I'm young enough to be your daughter. And that's just fucking gross."

Brunelle forced a smile. "Um, right. Sorry. That wasn't where I was headed with that. Not interested."

The bartender cocked her head, then put her hands on her hips and stood up straight, showing off her large breasts and curvy frame. "Oh, yeah? Why not?"

Brunelle's smile actually became a bit more genuine. He

enjoyed an unscripted question and answer exchange. It's what he did for a living. "First, as you mentioned, fucking gross. Second, I have other interests right now."

The bartender smiled at the first reason, then nodded at the second. "Mm-hmm. And what kind of interests?" She leaned onto the bar. "Nothing illegal, I hope? You totally look like a cop, so I know you're not."

Brunelle chuckled. "Yes, something illegal. And no, I'm not a cop." He savored the dramatic pause. "I'm a prosecutor."

Bartender stood up. "A prosecutor?"

"Homicide prosecutor," Brunelle added.

Bartender crossed her arms. "Homicide? Like murder? Sorry, mister, no murders here lately."

Brunelle took a sip of his beer. "I know. The murder was in Madison Park."

Bartender laughed. "Not too many people from Madison Park come here."

"No, the murder was in Madison Park," Brunelle explained. "But the murderer came here."

The bartender shifted her weight. She had abandoned her statuesque pose, but still cut an attractive figure behind the bar. Brunelle admired the long black hair flowing behind her shoulders as she processed the information she was getting from him.

"Lot a people come here," she said finally. "What's your name, prosecutor man?"

"Dave Brunelle. What was yours again?"

She ignored his question. "Well, Mr. Brunelle, like I said. Lots of people come here. So I'm sure I can't help you."

"Arpad Karpati." Brunelle figured if this guy was as much of a psychopath as he seemed, he would have made an impression on her, and everybody else.

The barmaid didn't respond immediately, but Brunelle examined her body language. She crossed her arms again and shifted all her weight onto her back leg. She dropped her chin just a bit. "Don't know him."

She was lying. That was obvious. The question Brunelle needed to figure out was why. The two most likely candidates were protecting him and afraid of him. Preserving the sanctity of bartender-barfly confidentiality was a close third. What's said in Darkness stays in Darkness. He'd start with that one.

"I suppose you two were friends, so I won't ask you to tell me anything he said. I just wanted to see what this place looked like."

"We weren't friends," the bartender was too quick to respond.

That didn't actually eliminate the third option. In fact it kind of strengthened it. It weakened the first one, though. She probably wasn't trying to protect him. But she might still be afraid of him, and she might still want Darkness to stay the kind of place people can come to without worrying that the hot bartender is going to tell everything to the cops. Or worse, the prosecutor.

Time to explore those options, with a single statement. Not even a question.

"He's in jail and he can't bail out."

The barmaid didn't say anything at first. She pursed her lips and stared down her small nose at Brunelle.

"You gonna get him?" she asked finally.

Brunelle shrugged. "Depends. He lawyered up, so I have to prove it through other witnesses. That's why I'm here."

One of her eyebrows rose. "You want me to be a witness against a murderer you're not sure you can convict?"

Brunelle smiled. Actually, he wanted her to direct him to

other witnesses. But she'd just given away that she had information. Why else would she think she might be a witness?

"You say that like it's a bad thing," he joked.

"Sounds pretty bad to me. I'm not a snitch."

"Bad for business, huh?"

"Bad for my fucking health," she shot back. "Fuck business. I don't want to get killed."

And Brunelle had his answer.

Now he could give the appropriate assurances. No use insisting the business would be okay if what she was really worried about was a bullet in her skull.

"He's charged with aggravated murder in the first degree." Brunelle knew it sounded impressive, but it was the translation into normal-speak that mattered. "It's a death penalty case. The only way he gets out again is on a bodyboard."

"Unless he gets acquitted," Bartender countered.

Brunelle grimaced. That was the rub. "Exactly. So I need to make sure that doesn't happen. That's why I'm here."

The brunette looked down at him, her eyes narrowed, but the indecision was still discernible in them.

"Help me make sure he doesn't get out again," Brunelle implored. "Help me hold him accountable."

The bartender stared at Brunelle for what seemed like the longest time. Then she smiled and leaned down on the bar opposite him. Brunelle managed not to look directly at her breasts hanging above the bar top, but only because he was so completely distracted by her running her fingers through the hair above his ear.

"Sorry, Mr. Prosecutor," she breathed. Sweet beer breath, so close he could practically taste her tongue. "I'm no snitch. And I'm not stupid either."

Brunelle's heart dropped as she pulled away, and not just

because she had rebuffed his best attempt. "Oh well," he managed to shrug. "I expected as much."

He pulled his wallet from his pocket and extracted some bills. "Thanks anyway." He set the money under the beer. "And for the record, I never thought you were stupid."

He stood up and turned toward the door.

"Hey, Mr. Prosecutor?"

Brunelle turned around.

"Faust," she said.

Brunelle cocked his head. "Pardon?"

"Faust," she repeated. "My name is Faust."

Brunelle smiled. "Of course it is."

CHAPTER 16

"You smell like beer." Kat wrinkled her nose at Brunelle as he stepped into the high school lobby. "You need a drink to sit through Swan Lake?"

"Probably," laughed Brunelle. "But no, I just had to stop by a bar to talk to a woman about a case."

Kat raised an eyebrow. "A bar? A woman? I don't need to hear about that," she laughed. "But don't try to tell me it was about a case."

Brunelle shook his head. "No, really. The Montgomery murder. Our murderer hung out at the bar. Just seeing if he said anything to anybody."

"Ahh," Kat replied. "And you had to drink a beer to ask that question?"

"I bought a beer," Brunelle defended, "because I wanted to talk to the bartender."

"The cute woman?"

"Right," Brunelle answered. Then he realized, "I never said

she was cute."

Kat smiled. "You just did."

She looped her arm through his. "Come on, lover boy, the overture is about to start."

Glad for the change in subject, Brunelle accepted her arm. "Well, let's go then. I don't want to miss any dancing."

Kat stopped short, pulling Brunelle to a stop as well. "You don't know anything about ballet, do you?"

Brunelle grinned. "Nope. But I'm here anyway."

Kat smiled. "Oh, good answer, Mr. Brunelle."

She kissed him on the cheek, then handed their tickets to the usher and they went inside to find their seats.

***

"Four acts?" Brunelle ran his hands through his hair three hours later as they waited for Kat's daughter to come out from backstage. "I thought you were only allowed to have two acts."

Kat laughed. "Allowed? Oh, Mr. Brunelle, you *are* a prosecutor."

Brunelle grinned. "It might not have been so bad if I'd had any idea what was going on. Aren't there supposed to be supertitles or something?"

"That's opera, culture boy," Kat shook her head. "In ballet, the dancing tells the story."

"Well, I think I need a translator," Brunelle joked.

"Allow me!" It was Lizzy, running up on tip toe, stage make-up still on and hair still pulled back into a lacquered bun. "I totally know the whole story."

Brunelle looked to Kat.

"Whatta ya say, David?" she asked. "Want to hear the story of Swan Lake?"

Brunelle hesitated. He actually was curious after watching

the entire story, like a television show in another language. Kat and her daughter sensed the hesitation.

"Over ice cream, of course," Lizzy added. "We always go out for ice cream after a show."

Brunelle smiled. "Well, I can hardly say no to ice cream, can I?"

They walked out to the parking lot and as they all settled into Kat's car, Lizzy tapped Brunelle's shoulder from the back passenger seat.

"So, are you mom's new boyfriend?"

Before Brunelle could overcome his shock, Kat started laughing. "We'll see how this ice cream and ballet thing goes, first."

***

"All right, all right," Brunelle was saying earnestly, small pink ice cream spoon pointed at Lizzy for emphasis. "So Odette is really a princess, but during the day she has to be a swan because of an evil spell?"

"Exactly," Lizzy answered. "Her and all her princess handmaiden people."

"And how many of those are there?" Brunelle asked, digging for more toffee caramel crunch.

Lizzy laughed. "Depends how many girls are in the studio. But usually a whole bunch so the dancing looks cool."

Brunelle nodded as he swallowed. "Okay, and the bad guy, what's his name again?"

"Rothbart," Lizzy answered. "He's an evil sorcerer who cast the spell on all of them."

"But why?"

Lizzy shrugged. "I don't know. Power? Control? Maybe just 'cause he's a dick?"

"Lizzy!" Kat yelled, but there was a smile not quite hidden

in the corner of her mouth.

Lizzy just rolled her eyes at her mother. "Anyway, yeah, that's why he gets so mad when it looks like Sigfried is gonna break the spell."

Brunelle frowned. He was interested in the story, but had no idea how the ballet had told it. "How does he break the spell?"

"Well, he doesn't," Lizzy answered. "The spell will be broken if he pledges his undying love to Odette, but he screws it up."

"I thought he did that at the party scene." Brunelle recalled the dancer on one knee pantomiming giving his heart to the beautiful princess. "When Odette was dressed all in black."

Lizzy and Kat both just stared at him for a second.

Lizzy turned to her mother. "Where did you dig him up, mom?"

Kat narrowed her eyes at Brunelle. "I thought you said you saw 'Black Swan'?"

Brunelle grinned. "I wasn't really paying attention to the plot."

Kat rolled her eyes and Lizzy giggled at her mom.

"That wasn't Odette, Sherlock," Kat growled. "You might have caught that if you hadn't been looking at—"

"Of course it was Odette," Brunelle drew on his courtroom experience to block the next words. "It was the same dancer."

"Right," Lizzy agreed, returning momentarily to her ice cream. "But she was playing a different part. Odile, an evil twin of Odette, created by Rothbart to trick Sigfried."

Brunelle almost dropped his spoon. "Oh. Oh, my God."

Kat laughed at her date. "Pretty evil, huh?"

"No," Brunelle replied. "Brilliant."

"Brilliant?" scoffed Lizzy. "He's the bad guy."

"Yeah," Brunelle smiled. "But what if the good guy did it?"

He raised an eyebrow at Kat and motioned toward Lizzy. "Whattaya think? Her voice is a dead ringer for Holly."

"Holly?" Kat's eyes flew wide. "The girl from the reports? Oh, no, David Brunelle. No, no, no, no!"

Brunelle tried to turn on the charm. "So you'll consider it?"

Kat's wide eyes narrowed into angry slits. "I can't believe you'd even suggest something like that!"

Lizzy reached out and placed a hand on her mother's arm. "What is it, mom? Is there something I can do to help?"

Kat spun to face her daughter. "You are not, repeat *not*, going into the King County Jail pretending to be the girlfriend of some homicidal maniac in the hopes that he says something incriminating to you."

Lizzy's face squished into a frown, but she didn't try to argue any more. So Brunelle did.

"Odile did it," he tried.

Kat's scowl melted, despite her obvious effort to stay angry. "You idiot. Odile was the evil twin, created by the bad guy, to defeat the heroes."

Brunelle smiled back. "Yeah, but otherwise it's a great analogy."

Kat crossed her arms. "Mr. Brunelle," she said evenly, "you promise me right now you will not send my daughter into jail wearing a wire to get a confession from that psychopath."

Brunelle took a deep breath, then sighed. He raised his right hand. "I promise."

Kat nodded. "Good."

Brunelle looked at Lizzy. She shrugged at him. But instead of shrugging back, Brunelle smiled, and winked.

CHAPTER 17

It was a bad idea, he knew. But it was better than the no ideas he had otherwise. Karpati was going to walk. They had no evidence against him other than Holly's testimony. But Holly wasn't going to talk, which meant Karpati would be on the street in a matter of weeks. There weren't even jail calls between them. None they could find anyway. She was just that damn scared of him. Without Chen and McCall browbeating her—something Judge Quinn was highly unlikely to allow—Holly wasn't going to say anything.

Brunelle couldn't even hope for a vengeful jury ready to convict with insufficient evidence. The judge would never let it get that far. Motion to dismiss granted, a murderer on the street, a girl in prison for something someone else did, and a smarmy defense attorney slapping him on the back on his way to his next big fee.

Which is why when his phone rang that Monday afternoon, Brunelle listened, considered his options, and then—against his better judgment—said, "Yes."

CHAPTER 18

"Thanks again for offering to do this, Lizzy," Brunelle said the next afternoon as they stood in the jail lobby, waiting to be buzzed inside.

"I'm kinda surprised you said yes," Lizzy replied. "You promised mom you wouldn't do it."

"I promised her you wouldn't wear a wire," Brunelle replied. "Which is true. We're not gonna have you walk up to him and pretend you're Holly. He's not blind. We're gonna put you in the holding cell next to him and tell him Holly's in there. So, a wire wouldn't be any good for that anyway. Too far away."

Lizzy laughed. "Mom's gonna kill you."

Brunelle nodded. "You still sure you want to do this?"

"That's why I called you," Lizzy answered. "Mom told me what they did to that girl. If I can help, I want to help."

Brunelle was impressed by the girl's sense of duty and

altruism.

"Besides," she went on, "I wanna be a detective when I grow up, so being a confidential informant at fourteen will look great on my resume."

Or not.

Brunelle nodded. *Kids these days.*

"So," Lizzy beamed, "what's the plan, boss?"

***

"I assure you, officer," Brunelle could hear Karpati telling the jail guard over the speakers, "I do not have court today."

"You're on the docket, Karpati," the corrections officer grumbled back. "That's all I need to know. Now get into holding cell number three and be quiet."

"Would you mind telling me the nature of the hearing?"

It really pissed Brunelle off that Karpati could speak so politely. He was gonna be a good witness. Damn it.

"Says here," the guard flipped through his sheaf of papers, "'Motion to Join Codefendants for Trial.'"

Brunelle was watching the scene unfold via the closed circuit television cameras that hung from the secure holding cell area behind the courtrooms. It was poor quality video, filmed at a strange downward angle, but he was pretty sure he saw Karpati frown.

"I don't have a codefendant," Karpati protested even as they reached holding cell number three.

The guard looked down at his papers again. "'Holly Sandholm,'" he read. "Says she's on for arraignment in adult court too. They musta transferred her case."

Karpati frowned again as he looked down in thought.

The guard laughed. "Congrats, you've got a trial buddy. Now get in there."

He half-pushed Karpati into the small, windowless room, and secured the door. Then he turned down the hall and yelled, "Sandholm! Cell four!"

***

Lizzy walked confidently down the cement hallway to cell number four. Brunelle was impressed. Chen not so much.

"You sure this is a good idea?" he asked as they both hunched over the monitor. "She looks awful young."

"She is awful young," Brunelle answered. "But damn, she sounds just like Holly. If she sticks to 'Uh-huh's and 'Mm-hmm's, Karpati should buy it."

Chen nodded. "Welles is gonna be pissed."

Brunelle laughed a bit. "Good."

***

The cell door slammed behind Lizzy and now all they could do was listen, and hope Karpati said something stupid.

The whole gambit was based on some dubious psychological profile Brunelle had attributed to Karpati. Karpati was a control freak—among other things. That's why he'd hired Welles, the best of the best, and a control freak himself. As long as he was getting three hots and a cot and Welles was at his side for every court date, then he was in control. Like the psychopath in the movie, straight-jacketed and a hockey-mask over his mouth to protect the young cop. He couldn't move, but he was still in control. Polite and courteous and prepared to eat your throat out if the opportunity presented itself.

But control is all about knowing what's coming next. Take the psychopath out of his element, sever him from his expected lines of information (*Why hadn't Welles told him about this hearing?*), and the discomfort level rises. Control freak wants control back, and after all, he's still a freak.

"Arpad?" Lizzy whispered. Smart. A whisper would be harder to recognize as not Holly.

Karpati didn't reply.

"Arpad?" she whispered again, but louder so it was more of a raspy yell.

"Shut the fuck up," Karpati replied.

Lizzy waited a few seconds. "Sorry, I thought you'd know what's going on."

Nice. Appeal to that control freak vanity. Girl had a future as a detective.

Karpati only hesitated for moment before replying, "I mean shut the fuck up about the case. Don't say shit. They're trying to scare you into testifying against me."

"I am scared, Arpad." The whisper was working. She kept it up. And short sentences. Excellent.

"Don't be. You'll be fine. Just don't snitch me out."

If Brunelle had been impressed with Lizzy so far, he was amazed by the next level. She turned on the water works. Fuck detective, the girl had a future in Hollywood.

"My lawyer says I'll get life!"

"Shut up, damn it. Shut up!"

Control freak doesn't like crying. Brunelle filed that away.

"Just don't say shit and we'll both be okay."

"My lawyer says," Lizzy half-whispered, half-sobbed, "if I don't say anything, *you'll* be fine. But I'm going to prison for the rest of my li-li-life!"

Brunelle leaned toward the monitor. If this was gonna work, here was where it would work. Moment of truth. Chen leaned forward a bit too.

"Listen to me, Holly. You don't say shit. I tell you what to do and you do it. Period. That's how it's always been. You agreed to that. And nothing changes just because I'm in here. I say knock on the door, you knock on the door. And I say shut up, you shut up. Got it?"

Lizzy paused, being sure to produce a few audible sniffles.

"Got it," she whined. Then, improv-style, "I love you."

Brunelle saw Karpati's mouth curve into a smug grim. "Damn right you do. Now shut the fuck up."

Brunelle leaned back in his chair and gave Chen the thumbs-up to get Lizzy out of there. After Chen hung up with the corrections officers, he turned back to Brunelle. "So, what do you think?"

"It wasn't a confession," Brunelle smiled. "But it'll do. If nothing else, I've got an iron clad case of witness tampering."

Chen raised a finger. "Ah, but Lizzy's not a witness."

Brunelle's smile faded just a bit as he considered his inevitable conversation with the assistant medical examiner. "She is now."

CHAPTER 19

"You did what?! Are you fucking crazy?"

Brunelle had decided to tell his co-counsel first, figuring she'd take the news better. Apparently not.

"You sent a state agent to entrap an in-custody defendant who is represented by counsel and had specifically invoked his right to an attorney?"

Yamata shook her head, sending silky black bangs across her eyes. "My briefs may be exquisite, but even those can't cover your ass on this one."

Brunelle smiled. It was genuine, but he had to prop it up a bit in the corners. "The defendant—who is a murderous psychopath, by the way. Don't think that won't go into the judge's thinking. No one wants to run for reelection as the judge who let the girl-killer back on the street—the defendant made spontaneous statements to a confidential informant. They were not in response to questioning and therefore no Miranda warnings were required."

"Confidential informant?" Yamata laughed. "That's what you're going to go with? She was a C.I.? Okay, well, he was still represented by counsel."

"That's an ethical issue," Brunelle countered, "not an evidentiary one. The bar association may care, but it doesn't suppress the evidence."

"Well, I'm going to care too," Yamata answered, "when you get taken off the case because the bar pulls your license."

"I care too, Dave." It was Duncan. He was standing in the door, arm against the door jam, looking casual, except for the tired frown on his face. "We need to talk."

Yamata jumped to her feet. "I'll be going now," she chimed. She made no effort to conceal her 'I didn't know he was going to do this' gesture from Brunelle as she slipped past Duncan. Duncan just nodded. Then he sat down across Brunelle's desk.

"She's right, you know," he started. "I can't let you try this case if you get in trouble with the bar."

Brunelle nodded. "I know. I think I threaded the needle, though. She didn't ask any questions. Only statements. Everything he said was voluntary, so it didn't need Miranda and I wasn't really contacting him for the purposes of the professional conduct rules."

Duncan frowned. "Do you really believe all that?"

Brunelle shrugged. He almost did. "I'll have to. Karpati was gonna walk. Now I've got an inculpatory statement. And at a minimum, I've got him on a witness tampering charge."

"Attempted witness tampering," Duncan laughed. "It wasn't really the girl." Then Duncan frowned. "Who was it really? And how did you get her parents to agree?"

Brunelle's smile was now fully artificial. "Yeah, about that..."

CHAPTER 20

What bothered Brunelle the most was what wasn't happening. His phone wasn't ringing. He'd left messages for Kat at her work and cell numbers, but no call back yet. He hadn't been explicit in his voicemails, and he didn't know whether Lizzy had even told her, but the lack of a return call was eating away a bit at his stomach.

The other person who wasn't calling was Welles. There was no doubt that Karpati had told him what happened. It would take a minimal amount of checking to discover that no such hearing had ever been set, and that Holly Sandholm had never left the juvenile detention facility across town.

Brunelle had expected Welles to excoriate him the moment he found out. The fact that he hadn't meant the defense lawyer was using his time and talents on drafting up some impressive paperwork. A motion to dismiss, no doubt. Maybe a bar complaint. Probably both.

The day ended with neither person calling him. Brunelle checked the message light one more time on his desk phone, then stepped from his office.

He needed a drink. And a pretty face.

***

Darkness was about the same as last time, maybe a little slower. It was Tuesday after all, not Friday. Instead of three businessmen sharing a table, it was two. And instead of Faust, it was some young guy with a burgundy faux-hawk.

"What can I get you, sir?" At least he was polite.

"A beer," Brunelle replied, then clarified. "Whatever's on tap, I don't care."

Fauxhawk nodded and was back in a moment with the beer.

"Is, um, Faust working tonight?" Brunelle tried to sound casual. He was pretty sure he'd failed.

Fauxhawk looked at him for a moment, then winced. "Dude, really? You could be her dad."

Brunelle offered a pained nod. "Yeah, that's what I hear. Just wondering. Was hoping to finish a conversation we had last week."

The bartender took a moment to size up Brunelle. "You a cop?"

Brunelle laughed a little. "No." He decided not to elaborate. "Don't worry about it. It's nothing important."

He took a drink of his beer and thought about calling Kat again. Maybe she'd been in autopsies all day.

"Dude?" Brunelle looked up at Fauxhawk. "She'll be in at eight."

Brunelle smiled. "Thanks."

And he knew how he'd be spending his evening.

***

By the time eight o'clock rolled around, Brunelle was sure of two things. First, he'd had too much to drink. Second, he shouldn't have had Lizzy be a C.I. after all.

But when Faust strutted in the front door, he forgot both of those things.

She was even more attractive than he'd remembered. He knew it was the beers, but he pretty much didn't care. She was hot. The End. And he was only old enough to be her big brother, not her father.

But that was kinda gross too, so he shook his head and waited for her to step behind the bar.

"Evening, miss," he said when she got close. He thought it sounded classy. He hoped it did anyway.

A smile curved across her lips, which only reminded Brunelle of the rest of her ample curves. She put one hand on her hip, and raked the other through her thick black hair. "Well, hello, Mr. Prosecutor."

Brunelle smiled. He wasn't drunk. Just feeling good. Still he needed to watch himself.

"Come back to interrogate me some more?" Faust asked with a defiant eyebrow.

Brunelle shook his head. "No, I just needed a beer. Tough day at the office."

Faust frowned. "Same case?"

"Yeah," Brunelle nodded and took a sip from whatever number beer he was on. "But no worries. It'll work out."

Faust nodded too, but a far more thoughtful one than Brunelle could muster. "Okay, Mr. Prosecutor. If you say so." She thought for a few more seconds. "You gonna be here for a while still?"

Brunelle looked up. He had been thinking about leaving. "Sure. Why?"

That full-lipped smile returned. "I get off at two."

***

Two o'clock in the morning was an ungodly hour anytime. But on a Tuesday night—or Wednesday morning—it was even worse. Brunelle killed the six hours until Faust got off work by drinking too much and eating too little. He was drunk, and it kind of pissed him off. He didn't like getting drunk. He wasn't in control when he got drunk.

"Still here?" Faust purred as she stepped up to his table, her purse over her shoulder, ready to leave. "Good. Wanna walk a girl home?"

Brunelle pushed himself to his feet. "I assure you, madam, I am in no condition to walk."

Faust laughed. "We'll see what you're too drunk to do. C'mon, old man."

Brunelle considered making the old 'I resemble that remark joke' but stopped himself. Maybe he wasn't too drunk after all.

***

Faust only lived a few blocks from Darkness in a small set of apartments over some independent clothes boutiques. It looked nice enough from the outside. Brunelle was dying to know what it looked like from the inside.

As if reading his thoughts, Faust stopped on the steps to the lobby, keys in hand. "You're not coming up, lover boy," she said. "That's not why I asked you to walk me home."

Brunelle tried to hide his disappointment. "I figured as much," he lied. "So why did you ask? Just wanted to see if I'd say yes?"

Faust shook her head. That smile she usually kept tucked away in the corners of her mouth was nowhere to be seen. "I wanted to tell you something, but I couldn't tell you in the bar."

Brunelle smiled. At least the night wouldn't be a total loss.

"Hey!" a man yelled at them before Brunelle could ask Faust what she had to say. "Why you talking to her?"

"Oh shit," Faust said, scrambling to put her keys in the door. "You better get out of here."

Brunelle's head was still a bit fuzzy, but he could tell Faust was right. And if he hadn't been sure, the two other guys who stepped out of the shadows as Faust disappeared inside her apartment building made it crystal clear.

"You're in the wrong place at the wrong time, suit," one of them said.

"And with the wrong girl," the original one added.

Brunelle grimaced. He knew he was about to get his ass beat.

CHAPTER 21

"Oh my God!" Yamata stopped short in Brunelle's office doorway. "What the hell happened to you?"

Brunelle tried to smile, but his black eye, swollen cheek, and split lip made the expression rather painful. "I fell," he joked.

"Yeah, and he'll never do it again," Yamata understood the reference to recanting victims. She came in and sat down. "Seriously, though, what happened?"

Brunelle ran a hand through his hair. "Okay, it's kind of a long story, but basically I got jumped by a bunch of guys last night who took offense to my suit."

Yamata nodded, smoothing out the fabric of her own expensive garments. "I don't like your suits either," she deadpanned. "But I wouldn't kick your ass over it."

When Brunelle just stared at her through puffy eyes, she raised her fists into some martial arts pose he didn't recognize. "I could, but I wouldn't."

"I'm sure," grumbled Brunelle. "But anyway, that's the short version."

"What's the long version?"

"I was in the wrong neighborhood at two in the morning with the wrong girl. Some gang took offense to an old man in a suit being there. They roughed me up and told me not to come back."

Yamata considered the information. "Wrong girl, huh?"

Brunelle shut his eyes with a wince. "That's what you focus on?"

Yamata laughed. "That's the most interesting part. Did you call the police?"

Brunelle shook his head. "No," he laughed. "It was humiliating enough. I don't need Larry Chen coming out to laugh at me."

Yamata frowned. "First, they wouldn't send a detective for a simple assault. And second, he wouldn't have laughed at you."

"You just did," Brunelle pointed out.

Yamata smiled. "Okay, yeah, he would have laughed at you."

Just then, Brunelle's secretary walked in with some papers. "These were just delivered to the front desk. They're on the Karpati case."

Brunelle started to read the pleadings as Yamata picked up his phone and dialed. He was curious what she was doing, but was more concerned about the motion Welles had filed.

Or motions.

'Motion to Dismiss for Governmental Misconduct; Motion to Dismiss Aggravating Factors; Motion to Disclose Identity of Confidential Informant; Motion for Release on Bail.'

The attached briefing was an inch thick. Brunelle wouldn't

have been looking forward to reading it even if it hadn't been a diatribe on his own unethical misconduct, which he was sure it was.

The sound of Yamata hanging up his phone shook him from the pages.

"I called Chen," she explained. "You better talk to him."

CHAPTER 22

"Vampires?" Brunelle couldn't believe what Chen had just said. "Are you fucking kidding me?"

"Well, they're not real vampires," Chen defended. He offered Yamata a 'how dumb can you be?' glance. "They just claim to be."

Brunelle pushed back in his chair. "I get that, Larry. Thanks. But how is it, given our upside-down, vampire wanna-be murder, that you haven't mentioned this particular street gang before? What do they call themselves again?"

"The No-Bloods," Chen answered.

"Cute," Yamata said. She was standing by the door, arms crossed. "Are their rivals the 'Not-Crips'?"

"Naw," Chen shrugged. "They're not part of the real gang scene. They're just some kids who like to play dress up."

"Is that why you didn't mention them before?" Brunelle

asked.

"Yeah," replied Chen. "That, and they hadn't beaten your ass before."

"You think it's connected?" Yamata asked.

"No," Chen laughed. "I think Davey was in the wrong part of town chasing the wrong piece of tail."

Brunelle was surprised until Yamata explained, "I told him about the 'wrong girl' thing you said."

Brunelle nodded and put his head in his hand.

"Well, it's worth pursuing, don't you think?" he asked. "A pseudo-vampire gang that hangs out near the bar where Karpati met Holly?"

Chen frowned and nodded. "Sure. Why not?" Then he stood up and stepped toward the door. "I'm gonna run down to my office. I'll be right back."

When he returned he had a thin manila folder with some mug shots. "These are the ones we think are in the gang. Think you might recognize them?"

Brunelle shrugged. "Maybe. But shouldn't we do this the right way? With a photomontage and an admonition form first?"

Chen started to agree but Yamata cut him off. "No. Go ahead and ID them, but if this is related in any way to Karpati, you can't prosecute the assault."

"Why not?" Brunelle asked just before Chen did.

"Because then you'd be a witness," Yamata explained. "And you'd get taken off the case. No way I'm trying this without you."

Brunelle frowned and pushed back in his chair again. It made his back twinge where they'd kidney-punched him. "Good point."

"Well, you can still ID them," Chen suggested. "Then I'll go harass them. I'm sure they've committed some crime I can arrest them for."

"If not, plant something on them," Brunelle joked.

"Shh!" Chen pointed at Yamata. "Not in front of the newbie."

***

When they got back to the courthouse, Yamata went straight to her office to do some research Brunelle had insisted—over her objections—that she do, and that she keep quiet about. His mind was pulling together the pieces of the murder, the assault on him, and Welles' brief. His thoughts were immersed in the solution he was considering, so he was genuinely startled when he walked into his office to find Kat Anderson leaning against his desk.

"Kat!" He shook the thoughts from his head. "What are you doing here?"

Then he realized, and tried avoiding the coming storm. "Done already with your autopsies for the day?"

Kat offered a large and cold smile. "Slow day at the morgue, Mr. Brunelle," she said. "But that's okay, because I'm about to kill you."

CHAPTER 23

"I can explain," Brunelle started. He used his calm voice, which was probably a mistake, and held his hands out, which ended up being a good move when Kat picked up his coffee mug and threw it at him.

"Don't pull that lawyer-crap on me, David! I know exactly what happened."

Brunelle nodded and frowned. He'd just expected Lizzy to keep quiet, so he didn't explicitly ask her to. Mistake, apparently. "What did she tell you?"

Kat picked up his stapler and threw that at him too. "I said no lawyer bullshit, David. Don't pull this 'what did she tell you' crap, trying to figure out what I know. You tell me. You tell me what happened, what you did to put my only child's life in danger."

Brunelle grimaced. He hadn't really thought of it that way.

"She wanted to do it," he protested. "In fact, she called me."

Kat eyed the tape dispenser next, but instead set her jaw and met Brunelle's gaze with force. "Of course she did, you jack-ass. You showed her attention. Her own fucking father doesn't call except on Christmas, and even then it's at the end of the day. He sends a belated birthday card every year too, but that's it. Then some handsome adult male father-figure comes into her life and she's already planning our wedding. By the time she picked up the phone, you were practically her step-father in her mind."

Brunelle grinned. "Handsome?"

The tape-dispenser flew past his head.

"Don't joke about this, David. Not this."

Before he could reply, there was a light knock on his office door. "Is everything okay in there?"

It was his secretary. "Yes, Danielle," Brunelle answered through the door. "Everything's fine."

The lack of response suggested the legal assistant had accepted his assurance.

"Sorry." Brunelle turned his attention back to Kat. "Where were we?"

She crossed her arms and glowered at him. "You were about to explain how you've endangered the life of my baby."

Brunelle nodded. "Right. Well, see, this is what we did..."

He explained it all. From his initial idea, to his phone call with Lizzy, through working out the logistics with the jail, and making sure word didn't get out to Welles or Edwards. And he made sure to emphasize what a good job Lizzy did.

Kat shook her head. "That damn girl is such a performer."

"She's got a future as a detective too," Brunelle added. "She's got great instincts."

Kat smiled. "She's got tight lips too. Never breathed a word of it to me."

Brunelle's jaw dropped. "What? But you said—"

"I said nothing, dear lawyer," Kat grinned. "I told you to tell me what happened and you did." Then she couldn't suppress a laugh. "You big dummy."

Brunelle wanted to be angry at being tricked, but that thick black hair and those twinkling eyes wouldn't let him. "Well done, counselor," he said instead. "So how did you even know?"

"All over the news," Kat replied. "Welles filed a motion to dismiss the case because you used an unidentified teenage girl to trick his client into making inculpatory statements."

"They weren't that inculpatory," Brunelle shook his head.

"Focus, lawyer boy," Kat responded. "You used a teenage girl to trick him three days after you learn about Odette and Odile from my daughter. Didn't take a brain surgeon to figure that one out."

"Just a medical examiner," Brunelle joked.

"We're smarter than brain surgeons anyway," Kat replied. "I've cut up plenty of brains in my day."

"I'm sure you have," Brunelle answered. "Although making sure they still worked wasn't really a concern."

"Details," Kat waved away Brunelle's comment. She sat on the edge of his desk and picked up his letter opener, testing its weight in her hand. Brunelle felt the urge to duck.

"But you know what really bothers me?" she asked. She didn't wait for a reply. "You lied to me, David. You promised me you wouldn't do it, and you did it anyway. You lied to me."

Brunelle waited for the letter opener to fly at him, but it remained distant, but ready, in Kat's steady hand. He decided to choose his words carefully.

"I didn't lie to you, Kat. I meant it. I wasn't going to do it at all until Lizzy called me. Then I thought back on our conversation. What I promised was to not put a wire on her. And we didn't. We used the jail's surveillance equipment."

Kat looked him square in the eye. "Are you fucking kidding me? You're going to split hairs like that? I basically have a knife in my hand. It's dull, but that's just gonna make it hurt more."

She started to stand up.

"It's not an insignificant difference," Brunelle insisted. "If we'd done a wire, we would have needed a warrant and I would have had to identify Lizzy in the warrant application. But as it is, I can keep her identity secret."

Kat paused, letter opener still at the ready. "Her identity is secret?"

Brunelle sighed. "Well, yes. Of course. I'm not that stupid. She's identified in the reports as confidential informant #7. And that just means she was the seventh C.I. Chen used so far this year."

Kat narrowed her eyes. "But you can't keep it secret forever. She's going to have to testify, right?"

Brunelle shook his head. "No. This was never about getting a confession for trial. I can't send a C.I. in to talk to someone who's invoked his right to an attorney. Not and use the information for his trial anyway. No, this is about shoring up a weak case so the judge doesn't dismiss it."

Kat's narrowed eyes were joined by a doubtful frown. She pointed the letter opener at Brunelle. "Explain."

"Welles was going to file a motion to dismiss anyway," Brunelle answered. "Our case is paper thin. It's just and righteous, but paper thin. We can't call Holly and we don't have any other witnesses. But now Karpati has admitted to the murder—or at least to telling Holly to knock on the door. That's not going to convict him at trial, but it should keep the judge from throwing it out, now that she has confirmation, even through inadmissible evidence, that Karpati did it. Hopefully she'll let the jury acquit instead of tossing it out pre-trial. She doesn't want to be the judge who let the kid-killer out. Not in an election year."

"But if the evidence is inadmissible, how does the judge even know about it?"

Brunelle smiled broadly. "Because Welles put it in his brief."

CHAPTER 24

"Welles' brief is mostly bullshit," Yamata opined from a cross-legged slouch across from Brunelle's desk. He tried not to look up her skirt. "We don't have to reveal the C.I.'s identity if we're not going to use her."

"And we're not," Brunelle confirmed, being sure to address his co-counsel's face.

"We can't," Yamata corrected. "Not in this trial anyway. If you charge him with attempted witness tampering, then you'll have to, but not as it stands now."

Brunelle nodded. He'd pretty much figured that out already. "You said 'mostly' bullshit. What's not bullshit?"

Yamata leaned forward. She didn't uncross her shapely legs, but now her chest was competing for Brunelle's attention. He almost wished Duncan had assigned that irritating guy Peters to co-chair. But not quite.

"The motion to dismiss the aggravators is strong. He has affidavits from three doctors that the method of killing in this case doesn't rise to the level of torture. And he's calling bullshit on your burglary based on the homicide aggravator."

"You don't like that, huh?" Brunelle asked.

"No. It's weak. Weaker than weak. And the judge is going to dump it."

Brunelle chewed his cheek for a moment. "You're right, she is. What about the torture one?"

Yamata shrugged. "It's fifty-fifty, I'd say. Now you're talking about a factual determination: how much did she suffer? Not a legal question about whether a murder can be aggravated by itself. The judge is going to be more open to keeping that one alive, but it may be hard if he's got three docs who will all say she didn't really suffer, not more than any other murder victim anyway."

Brunelle nodded.

"Do we have any docs who could testify she did?" Yamata asked.

"No," answered Brunelle.

"Why not?"

"Because," Brunelle frowned, "she didn't."

***

Brunelle pushed back in his chair. His reply brief was done. He wasn't going to make Yamata write this one. She was good, too good to write what needed to be written in that brief. The set up for the other pleading he drafted.

He knew he was going to lose the aggravators. If he just let that happen, Karpati's sentence would drop from death or life without parole to twenty years. Still a lot, but not enough. The bastard was young. He'd be out of prison before he reached Brunelle's age. That wasn't acceptable.

It was well past the end of the day. Everyone else had gone home hours ago, including the legal assistants who sat near the printer where his documents usually printed. He pulled open his reply brief and his other document. He'd file the reply in the morning. The other one would stay inside the file until the hearing. He hoped he wouldn't have to file it. He really hoped that.

CHAPTER 25

"Are the parties ready on the matter of State versus Karpati?" Judge Quinn didn't look at the lawyers as she took the bench and called the case.

"Ready and eager to argue our cause, Your Honor," announced William Harrington Welles.

Brunelle expected the usual disapproving glance from the judge, maybe even a 'save it for the jury' comment. But there was nothing of the kind. That worried Brunelle a little.

He reminded himself that although there was no jury there, there was media. Several television cameras were filming the proceeding through the glass partition that separated the gallery from the secure courtroom.

"The State is ready," Brunelle stood to answer the judge.

"Will you be arguing for the State this time?" she asked.

"Yes, Your Honor."

"I noticed you wrote the brief, Mr. Brunelle."

"Yes, Your Honor."

"Ms. Yamata writes excellent briefs," the judge observed.

Brunelle managed a smile and sat down.

"Ouch," whispered Yamata.

"Bet it doesn't hurt half as much as her ruling," Brunelle whispered back.

"It's your motion, Mr. Welles," the judge announced, "so why don't you go first."

"I would be delighted," Welles puffed. "Shall I argue all my motions at once, or would Your Honor prefer to rule on them in turn?"

Quinn frowned. She didn't consult Brunelle. "What is your preference, Mr. Welles?"

"I would ask the court to rule on them in turn. I believe the court's decision on one may help the court in ruling on the next."

"All right then, Mr. Welles. Proceed with your first motion."

Welles grinned at Brunelle, clearly relishing the smack-down he intended to inflict upon his opponent.

"Then let us begin with our motion to reveal the identity of the state agent sent into the jail to illegally interrogate my client."

Judge Quinn finally looked to the prosecution table. "Is that all right with you, Mr. Brunelle?"

"Yes, Your Honor, although I disagree with the characterization."

"I just asked if you were prepared to argue that motion, Mr. Brunelle. Yes or no. You can argue the merits when Mr. Welles is finished."

Brunelle forced a smile and offered a compliant nod. "Yes, Your Honor. I am prepared for this motion. Thank you."

The judge looked back at Welles. "Please proceed, counsel."

"Thank you, Your Honor. As the court knows, my client, Mr. Karpati, is being held—over my strenuous and righteous objection, I might add—without the opportunity to post bail. He is in custody because, and only because, the State has filed these meritless aggravating factors, turning the outlandish accusation of murder against my client into the reprehensible charade of capital murder."

"I'm sorry, Your Honor," Brunelle interjected. "I thought we were arguing the C.I. motion, not the aggravators?"

"Don't interrupt," the judge snapped at Brunelle. He sat down again.

"We are so screwed," Yamata whispered. Brunelle just nodded as he pretended to take notes.

Judge Quinn turned back to Welles. "Thank you counsel, I am aware of your client's custody status and the role both the prosecutor and I have played in that. Could you explain to me why that's relevant to your motion to reveal the identity of the police agent Mr. Brunelle sent in to question your client?"

"Of course, Your Honor," Welles replied with a slight bow of his head. "Thank you for allowing me to make a full record. As the court is aware, any questioning of a citizen while that citizen is detained must be preceded by an advisement of Constitutional rights—the so-called Miranda warnings, although we all know there have been literally hundreds of cases since Miranda versus Arizona which have recognized, reaffirmed, expanded, and confirmed the right of someone whose liberty has been stolen from him to know, before an inherently coercive interrogation is begun, that not only does he have the right not to answer any questions, but he has the right to have an attorney at that very moment to help him decide whether to answer such questions."

Welles paused to take a sip of water. Then he laid a fatherly hand on Karpati's back and continued. "Your Honor, my client did both of these things when initially arrested. He requested an attorney and he declined to answer questions until he had an opportunity to discuss the case with someone trained in the criminal laws. And I can assure you," Welles went on, "that he made sure the detectives were paying close attention when he made that request."

Brunelle couldn't quite suppress a smile at the memory of Karpati yanking Chen's chain.

"And so not only do we have a situation where my client was in custody due to the unethical charging decisions of Mr. Brunelle, but even knowing from prior conduct of this particular man"—again a heartfelt pat on Karpati's shoulder—"that he wished to have an attorney present, his own attorney whom he had taken the trouble and expense to retain, nevertheless Mr. Brunelle sent in an undercover officer—there really is no other way to describe this person—an undercover police officer to question my client."

Another sip of water. Then a step behind his client and both hands on his shoulders. "That is beyond the pale, Your Honor, and we simply must be given the identity of this police officer so that I might properly prepare to defend my client's very life against the unlimited resources and power of the state. Thank you."

"Thank you, Mr. Welles," Judge Quinn nodded warmly. Then a cold expression as she turned to Brunelle. "Response?"

Brunelle stood up and cleared his throat. "It's very simple, Your Honor. The State does not intend to use this witness or any of the information gathered through this witness at trial. Therefore the informant's identity is not discoverable."

Brunelle waited for the judge to respond. She did. "That's it?"

"That's enough. Not a witness, not discoverable. That's the

end of the inquiry."

"Then why send her in, Mr. Brunelle?" Judge Quinn asked. "Surely you intended to use her as a witness. Should the fact that she failed to gather useful information relieve you of the obligation of divulging her identity?"

"She did gather useful information," Brunelle countered. "Mr. Karpati admitted to instructing Holly Sandholm to knock on the victim's door so they could gain access to the home and commit the murder."

"Objection!" Welles slammed the table as he stood up. "That is a complete misrepresentation of my client's statement. And furthermore, if the State has no intention of using the information at trial, then it's improper and unethical for him to provide that information to the media." Welles waved at the TV cameras. "He's trying to taint the jury pool."

Judge Quinn smirked at Welles familiarity with that concept. She looked to Brunelle. "Any response to the objection, counsel?"

"Just that I was answering a direct question by the court, not trying to taint the jury pool. We obtained information useful to this prosecution. We will not be using it. We will not be calling this witness. Therefore the identity of the witness is irrelevant."

"Then why send her in?" asked the judge.

"This was a heinous murder, Your Honor. And evidentiary questions aside, there is no doubt Mr. Karpati committed it."

"Objection!" Welles slapped the table again.

"Overruled," the judge said quietly. "Go on, Mr. Brunelle."

"Thank you, Your Honor. As I was saying, there is no doubt Mr. Karpati committed this heinous murder. It seems reasonable that this might not be the only violent crime he had committed. It also seems reasonable that Miss Sandholm might have helped in other crimes before the murder of the victim in this case.

Accordingly, we attempted to gain information, not necessarily about this case—for which I agree he was represented by Mr. Welles—but also about additional cases for which I am unaware Mr. Welles has been retained."

Brunelle turned to his opponent. "Has your client committed other murder you represent him on that we don't know about?"

Welles' face started to blotch red, but before he could reply, the judge said, "Direct your comments to the bench, counsel, not each other." She pursed her lips and raised an eyebrow at Brunelle. "You expect me to believe you sent that girl in there to get info about other murders, and not this one?"

Brunelle smiled. "I assure you, Your Honor. Had Mr. Karpati confessed to additional murders, we would be prosecuting those as well."

The judge nodded for several moments. Then she looked at Welles. "The defense motion to reveal the identity of the confidential informant is denied. The State has represented they will not use the witness at trial. I will hold them to that."

"But Your Honor," Welles protested, "we need to know her identity. We need to interview her. We need to—"

"I know what you want to do, Mr. Welles," Judge Quinn interrupted, "but I am not putting a juvenile in your cross-hairs if I don't have to. Next motion."

Welles was visibly shaken, Brunelle pleasantly surprised. While Karpati rasped something unpleasant in Welles' ear, Yamata offered her own, "Good job!" whisper to Brunelle. He just smiled, suddenly hopeful he might win the motions after all.

Welles stood up. "Yes. Well, then. Perhaps we should just move to the most important motion, the motion to dismiss the case for governmental misconduct."

Judge Quinn nodded. "And is the alleged misconduct the

same you just outlined for me in your previous argument?"

"Yes, Your Honor," Welles started.

"Motion denied," Judge Quinn interrupted. "Mr. Brunelle has articulated a legitimate law enforcement purpose for his actions, and I have fashioned a remedy short of dismissal. That witness shall not be allowed to testify at your client's trial. Therefore, dismissal is not warranted."

Brunelle smiled again. Two for two. The warm "Good job again" whisper from his attractive co-counsel only deepened the smile.

"Well, then," Welles stammered. "We would next ask the court to dismiss the aggravating factors alleged by the State. They are unsupported by the law or the facts, and should not be allowed to be put to a jury. The mere presence of these allegations will prejudice my client by suggesting his alleged crime was worse than others similar in nature. The court should dismiss the burglary aggravator because the alleged burglary is based on the murder itself. That is bootstrapping and completely unfair. Further, the court should dismiss the aggravator of torture for, while no doubt this was a heinous murder—apparently committed by the young lady in juvenile detention who confessed to it—"

"Now who's trying to taint the jury pool?" Judge Quinn interrupted.

"By no means, Your Honor," Welles replied, hand to his heart and apparently aghast at the very notion. "I simply point out the fact that there is no evidence that my client committed this crime, let alone that this poor girl suffered any more than any other murder victim. Accordingly, these aggravating factors must be dismissed, lest their very existence prejudice my client's right to a fair trial."

Judge Quinn scowled this time, her narrowed eyes trained

on the defense attorney. Then she turned to Brunelle. "Tell me why I shouldn't dismiss these aggravators."

Brunelle stood again to address the court. "Gladly, Your Honor. First of all, I disagree with counsel's characterization of the evidence for these aggravators as 'weak.' There is no doubt Mr. Karpati committed a burglary, and—"

"Let me stop you there, counsel," the judge interrupted. "How did he commit a burglary? Was anything stolen?"

"No, Your Honor," Brunelle admitted. Now he had to engage in that dance of educating a judge about the law without the judge feeling like she's being talked down to. "As the court knows, burglary is unlawfully entering a building with the intent to commit a crime. Here, Mr. Karpati forced his way into the victim's home with the intent to commit murder."

"So murder is the predicate crime for the burglary?"

"Yes, Your Honor."

"Nothing else?"

"No, Your Honor."

Judge Quinn nodded. "The defense motion is granted. I won't let you aggravate a murder with itself. The burglary aggravator is dismissed."

Brunelle was surprised despite himself. He had originally expected to lose that motion but the hearing had gone so well to that point, he thought he was home free. He glanced at the defense table. Welles looked a bit surprised too, but it was hard to see through his smarmy grin.

"What about the torture aggravator, Mr. Brunelle?" the judge pressed. "Any response to that?"

Brunelle gathered himself. "Well, this one is different in kind, Your Honor. The court just made a legal ruling that burglary by murder can't aggravate the same murder. I disagree, but I understand the logic. But this aggravator is a factual determination. Either the girl suffered to a degree associated with torture, or she didn't. Whether she did should be left to the sound judgment of the jury."

Judge Quinn raised an eyebrow. "Do you think I can never dismiss a charge if there's no evidence to support it?"

Brunelle pressed a hand into his pants pocket and raised the other in a professorial gesture. "Well, that's an interesting question, Your Honor. Allow me to suggest that the answer might be 'No, you can't.' It's a separation of powers issue. The prosecutor's office is part of the executive branch. We decide what charges are brought. Your Honor is part of the judicial branch and ought not to be allowed to second guess the charging decisions of the executive."

"But I just dismissed one of your aggravators," the judge pointed out.

"Yes you did," Brunelle acknowledged. "Over my objection, I might add. But that may be different. That was a purely legal question. This one is factual."

"But isn't there case law that a court can dismiss charges when it determines that no reasonable jury could find what the State is alleging?" the judge pressed. "State v. Knapstad? Bremerton v. Corbett?"

"Well, yes," Brunelle admitted. "But I don't think that's the case here."

Judge Quinn frowned and held up some papers. "Did you read the affidavits Mr. Welles provided?"

Brunelle swallowed hard. "Yes, Your Honor," he admitted.

"Do you have any affidavits to the contrary?"

Another swallow. "No, Your Honor."

Brunelle considered arguing the point further, but Quinn wasn't one of those judges who rules for whoever argues last. She was sharp. In fact, Brunelle was pretty sure she'd already made up her mind on all the motions before she ever took the bench.

"The defendant's motion to dismiss the torture aggravator is also granted."

Brunelle managed just to grimace even as the defense table erupted in hushed congratulations.

"We would like to be heard on bail, Your Honor," Welles trumpeted. "Now that this is no longer an aggravated case."

Brunelle didn't wait for the judge to ask his opinion. "We object to that, Your Honor. By court rule, all motions must be made with five days notice. That includes motions to reduce bail."

Welles huffed in surprise. "That's ludicrous, Your Honor. This is no longer a capital case. You can no longer constitutionally hold my client without bail. I shouldn't have to note a motion to be argued five days from now."

Judge Quinn glowered at Brunelle. "I understand the court rules, Mr. Brunelle, but why should we wait five days to do something that, Constitutionally, I have to do now."

"Because, Your Honor," Brunelle answered as he pulled copies of his pleadings from his file. He handed a copy to Welles and one to the judge, "the State is filing a motion to add a new aggravating factor. We can argue that in five days as well. If the Court allows the amendment, then bail cannot be granted."

Welles flipped through the document roughly. "New aggravator? Which one?"

"RCW 10.95.020, section fifteen," Brunelle answered.

Welles' face screwed up as his mind recalled the statue. "The gang aggravator? This wasn't a gang killing."

"It's any group, counsel," Brunelle explained. "It applies if the killing was committed to advance the defendant's status in any identifiable group."

"What group?" Welles demanded.

Judge Quinn looked up from her examination of Brunelle's pleadings. "Vampires?"

CHAPTER 26

The gallery broke out into almost immediate laughter. 'Almost,' because it took a second or two for everyone to confirm they really heard what they thought they heard. Even the jail guards were fighting back laughter. Brunelle scanned the courtroom. Yamata was staring at him in disbelief and Welles was grinning it up for the cameras. The only people who weren't laughing were the judge, and Karpati.

Brunelle made a point of never looking at defendants. Partly because he wasn't supposed to stare them down, partly because there was no reason to since all communication went through counsel, and partly because half the time they wanted to try to stare him down. But when he looked over to see Karpati's reaction, Karpati's eyes bored into Brunelle's. He could tell Karpati didn't think it was funny at all. The man was pissed. And that let Brunelle know he'd made the right decision.

"Order! Order!" Judge Quinn pounded her gavel, something judges rarely did in real life. "Everyone get a hold of themselves."

When the giggling subsided, the judge stared down at Brunelle. "Are you being serious, Mr. Brunelle?"

"Absolutely, Your Honor," Brunelle answered confidently.

"And why didn't you file this originally?" asked the judge.

"I considered it, Your Honor," Brunelle answered, "but there wasn't quite enough information to support it."

Brunelle waited a moment then glanced sideways at Welles. "That recently changed."

Welles decided to push on with the disbelieving laugh despite the judge's serious tone. "Really, Your Honor, this is farcical. Surely the court can see—"

The judge turned back to Brunelle. "Have you provided the defense with this new information?"

"No, Your Honor," Brunelle admitted, "but I can do that by tomorrow. I'm just waiting on some reports."

Judge Quinn narrowed her eyes again. "We'll set the motion to add the aggravating factor for one week from today. I will treat it the same as the torture aggravator, which means you better have some facts to back it up. Is that clear, Mr. Brunelle?"

"Crystal," answered Brunelle.

"Good," the judge continued. "And copies of any information, reports, whatever, that you intend to rely on must be delivered to Mr. Welles' office by nine a.m. tomorrow. Do you understand?"

Brunelle nodded. "Yes, Your Honor."

Before Welles could do more than shake his head and try another disbelieving laugh, the judge turned to him and said, "We'll set your bail hearing for the same time."

Welles threw a pained expression at the judge. "I object.

There are no aggravating factors at present, and this latest attempt by the prosecutor is beyond ludicrous. My client should be allowed bail now because—"

"I said one week from today, Mr. Welles," Judge Quinn interrupted. "Did you not understand me?"

Welles regained himself and dropped back into compliant attorney mode. "I understand you, Your Honor. One week from today. Thank you."

With that, the judge banged her gavel again and declared the court at recess. Welles stepped over to Brunelle, a smug grin on his face. "Pretty desperate move, Brunelle."

Brunelle smiled back. "Oh yeah?" He pointed past the defense attorney. "Your client doesn't seem to think so."

They both looked at Karpati, who only scowled back at them.

"I believe," Welles said after a moment, "that he's concerned about your mental health."

"He better be concerned about his own health," Brunelle replied, "because I'm planning on shoving a needle in his arm when this is all over."

Welles stared at Brunelle for a moment. "Very well, Brunelle. Those documents better not be even one minute late tomorrow morning."

"Don't worry, Billy. They'll be on time. I think you'll find them very enlightening."

In truth, though, Brunelle knew he'd find them reassuring. The vampire claim was almost as thin as the torture. It was going to be a battle to keep the case aggravated.

***

"Vampires?" Yamata finally asked as they walked into the attorney area between the courtroom and the hallway. "What the hell are you doing?"

"Whatever I can to keep this case capital," Brunelle replied. "You heard Chen. This guy is a wanna-be vampire."

Yamata shook her pretty head. "Maybe, but you've got no proof."

Brunelle shrugged. "Well then, we better call Chen when we get upstairs, and hope he's got something to back us up."

***

Getting upstairs proved easier said than done. When they opened the door to the hallway, they were met with the blinding glare of a half-dozen television cameras.

"Mr. Brunelle! Mr. Brunelle! Do you really think Karpati is a vampire?"

Brunelle squinted against the lights. "I really can't comment on pending cases. You guys know that."

"Come on, Dave," one of the reporters he'd come to know over the years tried, "you can't allege somebody's a vampire and then not give us a quote. You know this is gonna lead tonight."

Brunelle sighed. He did know that. And although he hated getting interviewed by the media, his boss didn't. And his boss had taught him two things: always have a quote ready, and never say anything that isn't already in a document filed with the court—that way anything you say is already out there anyway.

"The State is not alleging that Mr. Karpati is a vampire," he explained, "but we believe the evidence will show that he wanted others to believe he was and that he committed this murder in part to advance such a belief."

He knew that wouldn't satisfy them.

"Is that it, Dave?" asked the same reporter. "Can't you at least call him the 'Vampire Murderer' or something?"

"Sorry, Keith," Brunelle. "Just the facts." Then he spotted the door to the attorneys' area opening again. "But I believe Mr. Welles is about to come out. I'm sure he has much more he'd like to say."

The paparazzi sprinted toward the defense attorney as he emerged into the hallway.

"What do you think about your client being labeled the Vampire Murderer?"

Welles wound up for his undoubtedly eloquent and long-winded response. Brunelle didn't stick around to hear it. He had some getting-yelled-at to attend to.

***

"What the fuck were you thinking, Dave?" Duncan shook his head from across his desk. "Seriously, I thought we talked about this."

Brunelle had gone straight to Duncan's office for his whipping. He'd insisted Yamata come along, but only so he could make sure Duncan knew she'd had nothing to do with it.

"Maybe I should go?" she tried.

"No, Michelle," Duncan raised his hand. "Stay. You need to hear this too. Dave's dragged you into this mess, but I'm not gonna let him drag you under."

He turned his attention back to Brunelle. "You should have gotten my okay on this first, Dave, but we'll talk about that later. Right now, my phone is ringing off the hook. They're calling it the 'Vampire Murderer Case.' So I've got one question for you, and one question only: can you make it stick?"

Brunelle took a deep breath. He knew what he had to answer, but he'd made a career of being honest. He wasn't sure what the honest answer was, but he knew the right one. "Yes, Matt. I can make it stick. Judge Quinn won't dismiss this aggravator."

Duncan nodded. "Good. Because if she does, you're off the case."

Brunelle looked up almost as sharply as Yamata.

"And Michelle," Duncan went on, "you'll be lead. So be ready."

"Y— Yes, sir," she stammered. "Thank you, sir."

Then she glanced over at Brunelle. "Although I'm sure it won't be necessary," she said. "Mr. Brunelle, er, Dave, knows what he's doing."

Brunelle managed a smile. "Thanks," he said, even though they all knew she was lying.

CHAPTER 27

Chen's reports sucked.

To begin with, they didn't even come through the fax machine until almost five o'clock. More importantly, they consisted of little more than his interview with Brunelle about the assault. There was a paragraph about the general police knowledge of the No Bloods, but nothing specific. He'd sent an officer to round some up and interview them, but the officer "met with little success." There wasn't a single name of a single No Blood gang member mentioned anywhere in the report.

So Brunelle, after reading and rereading and rereading again all of the reports, was sure of two things.

First, what he had was never going to be sufficient to survive Judge Quinn. And therefore second, he was going to have to come up with something solid before nine o'clock the next morning.

He touched his still tender eye with a wince

"The things Lady Justice demands," he joked as he stood and took his coat from the back of the door. "At least she can buy me a drink first."

CHAPTER 28

Brunelle waited in the dark of the landing to Faust's apartment building. It was quarter past two. He'd had a bit to drink, but not too much. He needed to think straight. That would be hard enough sober. As if he weren't already sure of that, his heart quickened as he heard her boots tick-tack up the sidewalk toward him.

"Hello, Faust," he said from the shadows as she stepped onto the landing.

The brunette spun to face him, fear in her eyes for a moment—until she recognized him.

"Oh fuck," she exhaled. "It's just you. What are you doing here?"

"Just me? I'm hurt," Brunelle teased. "I'm also desperate. I need your help."

Faust slid her key into the lock. "A lot of men are desperate for me."

Brunelle tried to grin nonchalantly. "I'm desperate for information," he assured.

She pushed open the door and smiled sideways at him. "Is that all? Well, you can come upstairs anyway."

***

Faust's apartment was small, but classy, just as Brunelle had expected. To the left was a small kitchen immediately off the front door, with a living room and balcony beyond. To the right was the door to the one bathroom, and the short hallway to her bedroom. He couldn't help but catch a glimpse of the mirror opposite the bed.

"You want something to drink?" Faust asked as she latched the door behind them.

Brunelle was already in the living room, checking out the view from the balcony. It wasn't much, just the parking lot out back. "No, thanks. Er, sure. Well, I don't know."

"Awful late, huh, old man?" Faust teased. "Ready for bed?"

He turned around and met her warm gaze. "No," he insisted, despite the fatigue across his back. "Just want to get down to business."

Faust stepped into the living room and handed him a drinking glass of whiskey. "Mm, Mr. Brunelle, I like your style."

He felt his face flush. He tried to ignore it. "I mean my case. The information. I need your help."

Faust offered an intoxicating pout, then dropped onto her couch, crossing her strong-looking legs. "What information do you need, sir? I can't promise I'll give it to you."

Brunelle scanned the room. He skipped the arm chair and sat next to her on the couch. "Those guys who beat me up," he started.

"Oh, I'm so sorry," she interrupted. She reached out and

touched the bruise still half-visible on his cheek. "I shouldn't have left you there alone."

He smiled at her touch. "No, it's all right," he assured. "You were right to get someplace safe. But I need to know a couple things about them. My detective says they're part of some gang that pretends they're vampires."

Faust took her hand back and stared into her drink. "You don't get it, do you?"

Brunelle frowned in thought. He usually got things. "Get what?"

"You come walking into this neighborhood, in your fancy coat and tie," she reached out and took a hold of his dark red necktie, "pretending like you understand what it's like to live here because you read police reports from the safety of your desk. But when you get what you want, you leave. And I'm still here. I still have to walk home in the dark, hoping those bastards have someone else to hurt."

Brunelle looked into her dark eyes. She still had his tie. "I, I'm not sure about that. It's just, I have a job to do. That girl was murdered. I have to hold him responsible."

Faust set her drink down. "And I can help?"

"Yes," he almost pleaded. He set his drink down too.

She pulled him to her by his tie, stopping just before she kissed him. "Then you give me what I want too."

There was no way he could deny her. "Whatever you say, Faust."

She pushed him back onto the sofa and straddled him. She kissed him, long and probing, then pulled away again. "I say leave the tie on."

***

Brunelle squinted at the bedroom clock. It was 4:42. Faust

was asleep on his chest. She'd told him what he needed to know, between love-making sessions. Names of everyone in the gang, and confirmation that Karpati was one of them. Most of them were just faking the vampire bit, going along to scare people and to enjoy the drugs and women that gang membership brought. But there were a couple, like Karpati, who rode the vampire bit for all it was worth, insisting they really were vampires. And they really did need the blood of innocents. It left everyone in fear of them. Either they really were vamps, or, far more likely, they were nuts.

Thinking of riding reminded him of the woman in his arms. He'd need to leave soon, so he'd have time to type up what he learned and get it to Welles before nine. She seemed to sense his change in mood.

"You're leaving," she said without opening her eyes. It wasn't really a question.

"Not yet," he answered, stroking her hair. Then, he thought for a moment. "Thank you."

She chuckled. "Don't thank me. You don't thank someone for something they wanted to do."

Brunelle wasn't sure he agreed, but he wasn't about to argue with her. "Well, thanks for the information then."

He felt her nod against his chest. "I hope it's helpful."

"It was. The trial starts in two weeks, so I'll be sending you a subpoena."

This time he felt her shaking her head. "No, you won't," she replied pleasantly.

Brunelle considered for a moment. "No, really. I have to."

Again a soft shake of her head. "No, really. You won't. Use the information, but you'll find another witness for court."

"Why?"

This time she pushed herself off his chest. She swung herself over him and straddled him again. Her soft black hair curtained his face as he felt himself rise against her again.

"Because, lover. I'll testify I told you all that between the times I rode you and the times you fucked me from behind."

Brunelle blinked at her even as she ground down against him.

"The truth, the whole truth, and nothing but the truth," she purred.

He pressed up against her. "Okay then. No subpoena."

She just smiled down at him.

"Thanks, anyway," he managed to say between breaths.

She reached down and slid him inside her again, then she leaned forward and bit his lip. "I told you not to thank me."

CHAPTER 29

The courtroom was packed. Every seat in the gallery was full. TV cameras lined the walls. A good chunk of the defense bar and half of the prosecutor's office had come too. Including Duncan, who stood at the very back, arms crossed. Some probably thought it was to put pressure on the judge. Brunelle knew it was to see first hand whether the case fell apart.

Judge Quinn took the bench promptly and got right to business. Rather than argument, it was questions from the bench.

Yes, Welles admitted, he received the information by nine that morning. And yes, even though it was supplemented by official reports a few days later, there was nothing new in the reports. Brunelle had to admit the evidence was thin, and it might be difficult to secure the testimony of the other No Bloods, but he insisted there was an identifiable group Karpati belonged to and the murder could have elevated his status in the group.

Finally, Quinn announced she was done. "Okay, I believe I've heard enough. I'm prepared to make my rulings."

The courtroom buzzed for a moment then fell silent. Even Welles sat down and shut up. Brunelle gave Yamata a hopeful smile, but she just offered a nervous nod and looked back up to the judge.

"The first issue is the matter of the aggravating factor," the judge began. "The issue of bail is dependent, or at least impacted, by this initial question. So the question is: can the State prove that Mr. Karpati committed the murder to advance his status in an identifiable group?"

Brunelle bristled at the framing of the question, but bit his tongue. Quinn noticed his reaction.

"Or rather," she corrected, "is it possible they *could* prove it? Can they establish a prima facie case? That is, if I assume the truth of the evidence they say they'll present, and draw all reasonable inferences in favor of the State, is it at least possible that a reasonable jury could believe the aggravator?"

Brunelle appreciated the clarification. It was a lot lower of a standard. The jury might not buy it, but he should get the chance to try to sell it.

Quinn paused. "I'm mindful of my ruling regarding the torture aggravator. There, I found no reasonable jury could believe the aggravator. However, that ruling was based on the complete lack of evidence from the State that Miss Montgomery suffered more than any other murder victim."

She took a deep breath and looked down at Welles. "Here, however, the State claims they will present evidence that Mr. Karpati was a member of a street gang, that members of this street gang held themselves out as vampires, and that Ms. Montgomery died from an acute and apparently intentional loss of blood. I cannot find that no reasonable jury would find the aggravator proven. I have concerns about the underlying strength of the State's evidence, but if they prevail in convincing a jury that Mr. Karpati committed the murder, the jury must be allowed to consider this aggravating factor. The defense motion to dismiss the aggravator is denied."

Brunelle tried to keep his smile professional and not smug. And not betraying the overwhelming sense of luck and relief that washed over his insides. "That should take care of the bail argument too," he whispered to Yamata. "No bail on capital cases." His smile deepened. "Thanks to your exquisite briefs."

Before Yamata could whisper a reply, Judge Quinn went on.

"I do not, however, believe this controls the issue of bail."

Another buzz through the courtroom. Even Welles and Karpati looked surprised. Then Welles unfurled his own smile. Brunelle knew there was no reason for the judge to bring it up unless she was prepared to rule in Welles' favor. Every attorney in the room knew it, including Yamata. And Duncan.

"I am mindful of Mr. Welles' initial bail argument regarding the evidence being clear and the presumption great. The evidence here is not clear, and the presumption, as he said, is that the defendant is innocent of the charges."

Fuck, fuck, fuck, thought Brunelle. He doodled the word hastily on his legal pad, hoping this was just judicial masturbation, the judge waxing poetic on the law to show everyone how smart she was.

"I am also mindful, Mr. Brunelle," she paused and looked down at him; Brunelle met her gaze as neutrally as he could muster, "that the State only filed this aggravator after I had dismissed the others. Quite candidly, Mr. Brunelle, it was a move that smacked of desperation, and I am hesitant to deny a criminal defendant bail based on a last minute gambit of a desperate prosecutor."

Brunelle recalled his initial conversation with Duncan. He wanted to turn around and mouth 'told you so' to his boss, but decided better of it.

"Therefore," Quinn turned back to Welles, "I am going to rule that under the unique facts on this case, the court is permitted to grant the defendant bail despite the potential penalty in the case."

Welles stood up quickly, his face beaming. "Thank you, Your Honor. We suggest bail in the amount of—"

"Ten million dollars," Judge Quinn declared.

Welles was stunned for a moment. She pressed the advantage. "Just because I rule that he's entitled to bail doesn't mean I'm going to set a low bail. He's charged with aggravated murder, for Heaven's sake. Ten million dollars. Trial starts in one week. Court is adjourned."

The clerk called out "All rise!" and the judge disappeared into her chambers.

No one was quite sure who had won the hearing. Finally, after exchanging puzzled glances with Yamata, Brunelle shrugged and looked to Welles. "See you next week, counselor."

Welles' smile hardened into a determined grin. "Indeed. I shall look forward to defeating you. Again."

CHAPTER 30

"Me?!" Yamata gasped. "You want me to give the opening statement? No way."

"Sure," answered Brunelle. "Why not?"

"I said my briefs were exquisite, but opening?"

"Oh, come on. We both know behind those exquisite briefs is an even more magnificent opening."

Yamata blinked at him for a moment. "Please tell me you didn't just say that."

Brunelle could feel his face flush and he covered his eyes with his hand. "That's not what I meant. I just, um, that is..."

Yamata laughed. "I know what you meant. And thanks. But sheesh, watch your words, old man. That's how you end up getting sued."

Brunelle peered over his hand. A weak smile forced its way onto his face. "Heh, yeah."

There was an awkward pause while Brunelle composed himself. Then he cleared his throat and straightened his tie. "So, yes, anyway. I think you should give opening." He felt the blush again. "Opening statement. Make. You should make the opening statement."

Yamata chuckled again and shook her head. "And tell me, Mr. Brunelle," she leaned forward and purred exaggeratedly, "why should I 'give opening'?"

Brunelle managed to ignore the suggestion and answer the actual question. "Well, we're partners. Partners split the work. And I'm damn well going to do the closing argument."

Yamata grinned and pushed back in her chair. "Oh yeah? How come?"

Brunelle grinned back. "Because, partner, that's where you win the case."

***

Before opening statements, however, a jury had to be selected—no small task in a death penalty case. Luckily for Brunelle and Yamata, only jurors who promised they at least "could" impose the death penalty were allowed to sit on the jury. Anyone with an absolute moral objection to it—while certainly a defensible, by some a laudable, position in another setting—was excluded from the jury pool on the basis that they would refuse to impose the law duly enacted by the elected legislature. It was one of the few times the cards were stacked in favor of the State. In the end, twelve jurors were seated, plus two alternates—the suckers who had to sit through the entire trial, view all the horrendous evidence, then go home without deliberating, unless one of the regular jurors got sick or otherwise became incapable of proceeding. The fourteen of them more or less resembled the community, eight women and six men, eleven white, two Asians, and an African-American. Mostly retirees or Boeing workers—paid in full for jury duty by their conscientious good corporate citizen employer. A couple of teachers. And that one guy who said he was a consultant for some computer thing that Brunelle didn't understand. He figured Yamata did, but didn't want to ask. One, he didn't want to look stupid. Two, it didn't matter. The guy had a thirteen-year-old daughter. That was enough for Brunelle.

The big day came after the jury had been sworn in and admonished not to talk about the case, even with each other, until the evidence—all the evidence, from both sides—had been presented. No, they wouldn't be sequestered. Yes, there would be coffee every morning. No, they wouldn't be allowed to ask questions of the witnesses. Yes, they would be allowed to take notes. Thank you very much and we'll see you in the morning.

That next morning, Judge Quinn gave the jury some additional instructions, a little information about scheduling, and then said those words every prosecutor knows means it's time to stand and deliver.

"Ladies and gentleman, will you please give your attention to Ms. Yamata who will deliver the opening statement on behalf of the State?"

Yamata stood confidently and thanked the judge. She stepped into the "well"—the area between the jury box, the judge's bench, and counsel tables. The courtroom was packed again, at least half by other prosecutors who'd come to watch that month's "big trial." If Yamata was nervous, she didn't show it. She smoothed her suit, then raised her gaze and locked eyes with the jury.

CHAPTER 31

"A butcher," Yamata started. The room was silent save her voice.

"You hear that phrase sometimes when people talk about someone doing a sloppy job. 'She butchered that presentation' or 'He butchered that recipe.' And of course, when a surgeon botches an operation, she's called a butcher."

She frowned and raised a finger.

"But that description does a disservice to butchers. Butchers are as exact in their work as any doctor. As any lawyer, or engineer, or," she met eyes with the father-juror, "computer consultant."

A smile ventured respectfully onto Yamata's face.

"Think of the last really good cut of meat you ate. Maybe it was at a barbeque. Maybe at a fancy restaurant. Maybe just cooked up in your oven on a random Thursday night. Think about the skill that went into extracting that perfect piece of food from what had once been a live animal. An animal covered in hair and skin, with organs and bones and all sorts of things you try not to think about when you're eating a hot dog."

She shook her head.

"No, a butcher is a craftsman, someone who knows exactly what he's doing. Someone who knows how to kill an animal in a way that doesn't damage the prize of the meat. Who can skin and cut and dismember a beast until the only thing left are a series of plastic-covered styrofoam trays on a grocery store shelf."

Yamata paused. She had the room. Everyone was watching her, and she wore it like a silk blouse, like the lightest sun-dress.

"No, what makes a butcher isn't a lack of skill in the cuts, it's treating the thing you're cutting like a soulless animal. Like nothing more than the hunk of meat you see it as, existing only to provide sustenance to you and others. Having no value to anyone except the value of the life-force to be stolen and exploited and utterly consumed by the cutter."

She turned and pointed at Karpati.

"Arpad Karpati is a butcher."

Brunelle turned to see Karpati's reaction. The entire courtroom did, even the judge. He stared straight through Yamata, his anger blotching his face. Brunelle figured he couldn't be angry at the description; it was true. He was angry at being called on it and damned for it in public.

Welles was the only person who hadn't looked at Karpati. He was calmly jotting notes on his legal pad, seemingly oblivious to Yamata's words.

"Emily Montgomery," Yamata turned back to the jury. Her voice modulated perfectly from the righteous indignation to heartbroken empathy. "Emily Montgomery was thirteen years old."

Yamata didn't meet the father's eyes this time; that would

have been obvious. Her words would reach him just fine.

"She liked to roller-blade and walk her dog. Her favorite flavor of ice cream was vanilla and her favorite color was purple. And even though she never would have told her friends, she still kind of liked Barbie and kept all her dolls and doll clothes hidden in her closet."

Yamata paused again, as the gravity of the impending description began to settle over the room.

"And she liked to help people."

Another pause, this time from an apparent lump in Yamata's throat.

"And that turned out to be the death of her. Her innocence. Her openness. All the things we wish we could be. Good, kind, hopeful, selfless. Noble. The things that we all grew up and learned not to be. Because of people like Arpad Karpati. But Elizabeth was still too young, too pure, too good, to know what fate awaited her when she befriended a troubled girl named Holly Sandholm."

Yamata picked up a water cup from the spot she had purposefully selected on the prosecution table and took a sip.

"Holly was a troubled teenager. A young girl who'd had a rough life, made some bad choices, and hung with the wrong crowd. She ended up in juvenile hall. Theft and drugs mostly. Now, juvenile justice is all about rehabilitation. About attempting to save at least some of these kids. To turn them back onto a good path. Maybe not the straight and narrow, but at least away from the highway to prison so many of them are on.

"So along the way, one of the judges ordered Holly to do some community service work. She could pick any non-profit agency. She picked a church. Emily's church."

The jurors were all watching Yamata as she stepped again to the well. She wasn't pacing; that would have been distracting. But she took a single step toward the jury box as she started to bring the story together.

"Holly met Emily at the Westgate Christian Church one Sunday while she was doing her hours and Emily was staying after to help out. They were doing the same work, but for different reasons. Holly, because she had to. Emily, because she wanted to. Emily reached out to the new girl. They talked. Even across the gulf of their life experiences, they had things in common. They saw each other again over the next few weeks. And eventually they became friends.

"Or so Emily thought.

"What Emily Montgomery didn't know about—*who* she didn't know about—was Arpad Karpati. Because when thirteen-year-old Emily Montgomery went home to her pink-painted bedroom in her suburban home, fifteen-year-old Holly Sandholm went home to Arpad Karpati's bedroom in his downtown apartment."

Brunelle smiled. Perfectly delivered. Don't spell out the child rape allegation, they'll get it.

"He controlled Holly. Through promises and drugs, sex and fear. The same fear he tried to illicit in everyone else he met. Holly would do anything for him. Anything. And he needed her help to make sure the others in his life would be just as scared of him as she was."

Yamata had avoided looking at Karpati through this description, but she opened her shoulders just a notch in his direction as she continued.

"Arpad Karpati ran with a gang. A street gang. But not just any gang. Not Crips and Bloods and 'Gangland' TV specials on digital cable. He ran with a gang that claimed to be vampires."

This was the hard part. The jurors all either cocked a head, or leaned back, or crossed their arms—signs of disbelief. Signs that Yamata would lose them if she didn't play this just right.

"Yes, I said vampires. No one would believe that, right? And if no one believes it, no one is scared, right? So there's one thing to do: make them believe it. Drink the blood of a virgin. Drink the blood of Emily Montgomery."

A sob from Mrs. Montgomery punctuated Yamata's sentence and the crossed arms and cocked heads relaxed. The jury wanted more information. Yamata gave it to them. But not through the eyes of a lawyer, or even a cop. Through the eyes of a parent.

"When Janet and Roger Montgomery came home from dinner that night, their front door was unlocked. On it was a sticky note. It said, 'Don't go inside. Call 911 and wait for the police.'

"No parent in the world would have waited outside. But when they opened the door, their world shattered. Their daughter Emily had been murdered. Sweet, young, innocent Emily had been bound and trussed upside down—like a carcass in a meat locker— hanging from the stair railing, pale as the ghost she had become. Had become at the hands of Arpad Karpati."

She didn't look at him. She didn't have to.

"The only injury was a small slit to her throat, right into the carotid artery. She bled out, the way butchers kill animals. And like those butchers, Karpati the Butcher collected her blood in a bucket, which he took with him to prove he was who, and what, he said he was."

Yamata paused again. She sighed a deep, repulsed sigh.

"Emily Montgomery is dead because of one man. That man." She pointed but didn't look. "Arpad Karpati. And at the end of this trial, at the conclusion of the evidence, we are going to stand up again and ask for justice for Emily, ask for the only just verdict in this case: guilty.

"Thank you."

The room took a moment to relax from Yamata's grip. The spectators started breathing again and after a moment a few of the jurors shifted in their seats. It even took a moment for Judge Quinn to move to the next order of business.

"Mr. Welles." She looked down at him. "Does the defense wish to present its opening statement now, or reserve until the close of the State's case-in-chief?"

Welles stood up and smiled at the judge. "The jury will remember what the State promised here, Your Honor, and what they will inevitably fail to deliver by way of actual evidence. The defense will reserve its opening statement."

Quinn held her scowl in check in front of the jury, but Brunelle had more trouble. It wasn't just that Welles had managed to both reserve and give a micro-opening with his comment. It was that, damn him, he was right. Yamata had given a fantastic opening. Now they had better deliver.

CHAPTER 32

"Call your first witness," Judge Quinn instructed Brunelle.

The first witness. This was always one of the most important decisions in trial practice. Who do you start with? The lead detective, to explain the investigation? The first cop who arrived, to describe the crime scene? The medical examiner, to explain the cause of death? Yamata had suggested all of those, but Brunelle shook his head each time. Every case is different and the facts of each case tell you who to call first. In this case, with these facts, there was really only one person to call first.

Mom.

Janet Montgomery looked up at the judge, raised her right hand, and swore to tell the truth, the whole truth, and nothing but the truth.

Brunelle had everything ready. He made sure the box of tissues was not on the witness stand, but rather on his table, so he could get them for her in front of the jury. He had all the photos lined up on the counter in front of the court reporter. He started with the "in life" of a smiling Emily, hugging a puppy in the park on a sunny spring day. He left it up on the projector as Janet told the jury about her wonderful daughter.

Then a photo of the house. Not on a sunny spring day, though. That night. Dark, lit up by red and blue police car lights.

That's when he got to give her the tissues.

Then the photo of the note on the front door. Blown up, nice and big, on the screen. There wasn't a person in that jury box who wouldn't have been terrified to come home to that note on their door.

The only photo left to show was Emily hanging upside down just inside that door. Dead, thanks to Arpad Karpati.

Everybody knew that was the next photo.

And Brunelle didn't show it to her. Because you don't do that to a mom.

Mom told the jury who Emily had been. Let the cops tell them who she was now.

"Thank you, Mrs. Montgomery." Brunelle nodded to her, then looked up to the judge. "No further questions."

He sat down and got a "Great job" whisper from Yamata. It had gone perfectly. He'd extracted all the information he needed, and done so respectfully. His care and discretion just underlined for the jury how terrible the crime was, how unfathomable the loss. The smallest smile crept into the corner of his mouth furthest from the jury box.

"Let's see what Welles does with that," he whispered back.

Some defense attorneys start with an apology "for your loss" or something equally transparent. Not Welles. He had one question. One perfect question.

"You don't really know whether my client killed your daughter, do you?"

Her hesitation was its own answer. Before she could blurt out the 'Yes!' that she wanted to say, Welles interrupted.

"I understand, Mrs. Montgomery, that people have told you things, made promises and assurances. The police, the prosecutor. But you yourself, you have no personal knowledge whatsoever that my client is in any way responsible for the death of your daughter, isn't that true?"

Mrs. Montgomery shifted in her seat, but kept an icy glare locked on Welles. Finally, through gritted teeth, she admitted, "No."

Welles nodded, but knew enough not to smile. "No further questions."

***

And so it went, all day. Brunelle or Yamata leading the witness through their testimony, admitted photographs, pulling heart-strings. The first cop on scene who found the body, the paramedic who confirmed the death, the forensics guy who dusted for prints. And after every direct examination, one simple question on cross examination:

"You have uncovered absolutely no evidence that my client was in any way involved in the young lady's death, isn't that right?"

Brunelle got it. Back in his office at the end of the day, it was clear Yamata didn't.

"I think it went pretty well today," she said. "I don't think Welles objected even once."

Brunelle laughed sardonically. "Why should he? He's killing us."

Yamata cocked her head at her partner. "You mean that

little, 'You don't know my client did it' bit? Please. The jury gets what we're doing."

"Maybe," Brunelle shrugged. "But the judge gets what he's doing. She'll dump this thing at half-time if we don't put on some evidence Karpati is the killer."

Yamata's incredulous frown deepened. "There's no way she dumps it. We're totally proving that girl was murdered in the most horrific way."

Brunelle shook his head. "Of course she was, but we've got to prove Karpati's the one who did it. There are judges who would be afraid to dump a murder case, who'd leave it to the jury to acquit. But not Quinn. She'll fuck us. If we put on a hundred witnesses and every one of them ends with, 'But I can't say Karpati did it' we're fucked. Case dismissed."

Yamata's confident grin was gone. She crossed her arms. "So what do we do?"

Brunelle drummed his fingers on the table. "We hope Chen does better for us tomorrow than everyone did for us today."

***

"Lawrence Chen," the detective identified himself for the record after being sworn in and sitting on the witness stand.

Brunelle was standing across the courtroom, behind the last juror. It was an old trial attorney trick. It forced the witness to speak up and look at the jury. "How are you employed, sir?"

"I'm a detective with the Seattle Police Department."

Then, after a brief verbal resume, years of experience and commendations received, Brunelle got to what really mattered. "Are you familiar with the investigation into the murder of Emily Montgomery?"

Chen set his jaw. It was probably meant to seem serious. Brunelle worried it seemed forced. "Yes," Chen answered solemnly.

"And was part of your job to identify the killer or killers?"

Chen thought for a moment. "Actually, I would say that was my only job. To identify the guilty party and arrest him."

"And did you arrest anyone for the murder of Emily Montgomery?"

"Objection!" Welles stood slowly, a bemused smile on his face. "Objection, Your Honor. This is absolutely outrageous. I'll give Mr. Brunelle credit for his creativity in trying to mislead the jury but—"

"Well, now I'm going to object," Brunelle interjected. "It's inappropriate for counsel to suggest I'm trying to mislead the jury."

"If the lie fits," Welles started, but the judge interrupted.

"Children, children." She looked over to the jurors. "Ladies and gentlemen, I'm going to excuse you to the jury room while counsel and I discuss the objection. Thank you."

The jurors looked at one another and shrugged, but they did as they were told, standing up and filing into the jury room. When the door closed, Judge Quinn pointed a firm finger at Welles, "You will stop the speaking objections immediately, Mr. Welles. Do you understand me?"

Welles threw his arms wide and offered his most innocent expression. "I was just trying to articulate the basis for my objection."

"Don't bullshit me, Mr. Welles. It won't work. You just told the jury that the prosecutor was lying to them. You do that again, you're in contempt. Do you understand?"

Welles' face traded innocence for understanding. "Of course, Your Honor."

Before Brunelle could fully form his own 'told ya so' expression, the judge turned her finger to him. "And you. Stop lying to the jury."

"Lying?" Brunelle stammered. "I'm just—"

"You just asked the detective what his job was. When he said his job was to arrest the killer, you asked him who he arrested. Tell me that wasn't designed to have the detective tell the jury that Mr. Karpati is guilty."

"Mr. Karpati is guilty," Brunelle replied.

"Prove it," Welles laughed.

"I'm trying," Brunelle answered.

"Well, you're not going to do it with impermissible opinions as to guilt or hearsay," Quinn instructed. "This detective cannot tell the jury what other people told him happened. That's hearsay. And the law is clear in Washington: no witness, not even the lead detective, can give an opinion as to the defendant's guilt. That's for the jury to decide."

Brunelle clenched his fists, but didn't say anything. There wasn't any response, and he knew it.

"I would ask the court," Welles said smugly, "to instruct Mr. Brunelle not to ask about whether my client was arrested. And further to sustain my objection in front of the jury when they return."

Judge Quinn looked to Brunelle. "I think I should be allowed to tell the jury he was arrested. It's just true."

The judge nodded. "It is true, but you've set it up that the detective has knowledge the jury won't get and he determined Mr. Karpati is guilty."

"Again, Your Honor," Brunelle implored, "he does have knowledge the jury won't get, and Mr. Karpati is guilty."

"And again, Your Honor," Welles said, "I move the court to prohibit any further questions regarding my client's arrest. He requested an attorney and made no statements, so there is no admissible evidence from the arrest."

Judge Quinn raised an eyebrow at Brunelle, inviting a response, but he just shrugged. "I've made my argument."

Judge Quinn smiled. "And I'll make my ruling. No more questions about Mr. Karpati's arrest. Is that understood, Mr. Brunelle?"

Brunelle shrugged. "I'm not Mr. Welles, Your Honor. I disagree with the court's ruling, but I will abide by it."

Welles opened his mouth to protest, but the judge stopped him. "Ah, ah, ah, children. No more bickering." She looked to the bailiff. "Bring in the jury."

The jury marched in and retook their seats. Once they were settled in, Judge Quinn announced, "The objection is sustained. Ask a different question, Mr. Brunelle."

Brunelle forced a smile. "Thank you, Your Honor."

But the truth was, lead detectives are hugely important outside the courtroom and mostly irrelevant inside. Everything they learned was hearsay, so they couldn't tell the jury what witness so-and-so said. They sent everything to the crime lab for testing, but only the scientists could testify about the results. So really, about all they could ever say is, 'I was the lead detective. I talked to some people. I sent some stuff to the lab. I wrote some reports.' Brunelle tried to drag it out a bit, make it more interesting than that, but soon enough his direct examination had concluded.

Brunelle's only hope was that Welles would ask Chen the same type of question. 'You don't have any information that my client committed the murder, do you?' That would open the door to Holly's statement and everything else the investigation had linking Karpati to the murder.

So of course, Welles stood up and said, "No questions, Your Honor."

Chen was excused and Brunelle was in serious trouble.

CHAPTER 33

"We're in trouble, aren't we?" Yamata asked when they returned to Brunelle's office at the end of the day. The problems with Chen had been repeated with the patrol and evidence officers who followed. They spoke to people and collected evidence, but they weren't allowed to relate the substance of the conversations or the results of any forensic testing.

"Yeah, we're in trouble," Brunelle answered as he fell into his chair and raised his fingertips to his lips in thought.

"Do we have any witness who can put Karpati at the crime scene?" Yamata asked, choosing to pace over sitting.

Brunelle frowned through his fingers. "I can only think of one."

Before Yamata could ask, 'Who?' Brunelle hit the speaker button on his phone and dialed a four-digit in-county extension.

"Juvenile detention center," came the voice over the phone.

"Transport desk."

"This is Dave Brunelle with the prosecutor's office," he said with a shrug to Yamata. "I'm going to need a transport first thing tomorrow morning to the main courthouse."

"The adult courthouse?" asked the officer.

"Yes."

"And what's the name of the juvenile?"

"Sandholm. Holly Sandholm."

CHAPTER 34

"What the hell are you doing?!"

Jessica Edwards was angry. Livid. Maybe even apoplectic. She was inches away from Brunelle's face, which under certain circumstances might not have been so bad. But 8:50 in the morning in Judge Quinn's courtroom on that case were not those circumstances.

"I'm calling your client to testify," Brunelle answered calmly, taking a half step back.

"She didn't agree to testify, Dave. You can't do this."

"I didn't say," Brunelle crossed his arms, "I was enforcing a plea agreement. I said I was calling her to the stand. I don't need your permission to do that, Jess."

Edwards threw her arms up. "Of course you do, Dave. She's just gonna plead the Fifth. You can't call a witness just to plead the Fifth in front of the jury."

Welles, who, along with Yamata, had been content to watch Brunelle and Edwards have it out, spoke up. "She's right. I won't let you do that."

Brunelle glared over at Welles. "It's not really up to you. Last I checked you were still one of the attorneys, not the judge."

"It's settled law, my dear David," Welles replied. "You can't call a witness just to plead the Fifth Amendment. When the judge comes out, she'll ask, like she does every time she comes out, if the lawyers have anything before the jury is brought in. I assure you I will move to prohibit this charade."

Brunelle narrowed his eyes. He knew Edwards and Welles were right. But he also knew it was always easier to say you were going to do something than to actually do it. She might back down and testify after all.

And he had a Plan B. But both plans required Holly's butt on the witness stand.

"Fine," he said. "Bring out the judge."

The bailiff raised an eyebrow at him. The judge would come out when she was ready. But it was almost nine o'clock, so they didn't have to wait long before the bailiff called out, "All rise!" and Judge Quinn took the bench.

"Good morning, counsel. Any matters before we bring in the jury?"

Welles threw a sneer over at Brunelle, then a smile up to the bench. "Yes, Your Honor. It appears Mr. Brunelle has some theatrics planned for this morning. He intends to place Holly Sandholm—the one person who has confessed to this murder—on the stand for the sole purpose of having her invoke her right against self-incrimination in front of the jury. The idea is to bolster the State's unsupportable assertion in its opening statements without actually presenting any competent evidence. Obviously, this is improper and I would ask the court to prohibit it."

Quinn rolled her head to Brunelle and glared down her nose at him. "Please tell me this is a misunderstanding, Mr. Brunelle. You don't really think I'm going to allow you to do that, do you?"

Brunelle nodded politely. "I think it is a bit of a misunderstanding. Ms. Sandholm is here this morning and the State does wish to call her as a witness. It's one thing to say you're going to refuse to testify under the Fifth Amendment; it's another to actually do it. But we have no objection to the court having Ms. Sandholm initially take the stand outside the presence of the jury to see what she says."

Quinn stared at Brunelle for a few moments, then looked back to Welles. "Any objection to that procedure, Mr. Welles."

"I'd like to object, Your Honor," Welles laughed, "but I'd rather just get on with it. I have no doubt that Ms. Sandholm will refuse to testify. The sooner we can get this parlor trick over with, the sooner my client can be acquitted and go home."

"Well, I object!" Edwards stepped forward.

Judge Quinn raised an eyebrow. "Ms. Edwards. You represent Miss Sandholm, I take it."

"Yes," Edwards tossed back her straight blond hair. It was one of her signature moves. "I object to my client being transported here without any notice to me—"

"I left you a voicemail," Brunelle interrupted.

Edwards narrowed her eyes at him. "At seven-thirty last night. If I hadn't checked my messages first thing this morning I'd be in a completely different courtroom this morning."

"Ms. Edwards," the judge drew her attention back up to the bench. "Let's set aside the notice issues for a moment. We're all here now and I have a jury waiting. Is there any reason your client can't just take the stand and formally assert her Fifth Amendment rights?"

Edwards huffed and threw her hands wide. "Yes, Your Honor! She's scared to death of the defendant. She's a victim too. He raped her. The State even charged him with that before they dropped it for some reason."

"The reason," Brunelle stepped forward, "is that she refused to testify. Maybe she'll rethink it now that she's in a safe environment. Maybe we refile that charge."

"Well, now, I would object to that," Welles interjected. "Mandatory joinder rules clearly provide—"

"Enough, enough!" Judge Quinn raised her voice. The lawyers instantly silenced theirs. "There is no point in discussing who might object to what might happen if something else happens. Put Miss Sandholm on the stand and see what she does."

The judge nodded to the jail guard, who turned and opened the secure door to the holding cells behind the courtrooms. As they waited for Holly to be escorted into court, Yamata stepped up and whispered into Brunelle's ear.

"You told the family about this, right?"

Brunelle shook his head slightly. "No, there wasn't really time. Why?"

"Because the parents are in the gallery, and they're looking panicked."

Brunelle turned to see Mr. and Mrs. Montgomery sitting in the front row of the public seating section. They didn't look exactly panicked to him, but they didn't look happy either. Mr. Montgomery motioned for them to come over.

"What's going on, Brunelle?" he demanded when they did.

"I'm not going to let her off the hook quite so easily," Brunelle answered. "She can't just claim she's going to invoke her right to remain silent. We're going to make her take the stand and do it."

"Do we need her testimony?" Mrs. Montgomery asked.

Brunelle sighed. "Honestly... yes. It wouldn't hurt, at least."

"But what if she does refuse to testify?" was Mrs. Montgomery's follow up question.

"Don't worry," Brunelle assured. "I have a back-up plan."

"What's the back-up plan?" Mr. Montgomery demanded.

"The only way you get to claim the Fifth Amendment is if what you say would subject you to criminal penalties," Brunelle explained. "I can make that go away by giving her immunity."

The Montgomerys both stared at him for several seconds. "Immunity?" Mrs. Montgomery asked.

"Yes," Brunelle said. "I can do that unilaterally, even without an agreement. I do that, and she can't plead the Fifth any more."

Before either of the Montgomery's could say anything more, the guard brought Holly into the courtroom.

Brunelle excused himself with a shrug then returned to counsel table to watch Holly be marched up to the witness stand.

She stared straight down at her feet the whole time. As she passed Karpati's table he made a kissing noise, but by the time anyone realized what he'd done, Holly was sitting down. Edwards stepped over and whispered something into her ear.

"Mr. Brunelle?" Judge Quinn invited.

"Thank you, Your Honor," Brunelle replied. Then, turning to Holly, he started. "Could you please state your name for the record?"

"My client," Edwards said in response, "invokes her right against self-incrimination under the Fifth Amendment of the United States Constitution and Article One, Section Seven of the Washington State Constitution."

Brunelle shrugged and looked up at the judge. "She has to do it personally, Your Honor."

Judge Quinn looked down at Edwards. "Mr. Brunelle is right. She does have to do it personally."

When Edwards frowned, the judge went on. "I don't expect her to cite constitutional provisions, but she has to say herself that she's refusing to testify."

"I refuse to testify," Holly blurted out.

Edwards smiled. The judge did too. "Is that good enough for you, Mr. Brunelle?"

Brunelle shrugged again. "I think the question is whether that's good enough for Your Honor. Just let me know when you find it to be an invocation of her right against self-incrimination so I know when to go ahead and grant her immunity."

"Immunity?" Welles slammed the table as he stood up. "You're going to grant immunity to the only person who admitted to the murder?"

Edwards whispered hurriedly into Holly's ear. Holly sat up straight and said, "I invoke my right against self-incrimination. Under the constitution and stuff."

Judge Quinn crossed her arms and leaned back in her chair. She smiled slightly and looked down at Brunelle. "I can't tell the prosecutor's office what to do regarding immunity. I will find that Miss Sandholm has invoked her right against self-incrimination, and I rule that the State may not call her as a witness in front of the jury just to invoke that right again."

She leaned forward. "So what are you going to do, Mr. Brunelle?"

But before Brunelle could respond, Yamata tugged his jacket sleeve and pointed to the gallery. The Montgomerys were trying to get his attention.

"May I have a moment, Your Honor?" Brunelle asked.

"Of course, counsel. But remember, the jury is waiting."

Brunelle and Yamata stepped to the half-wall separating the gallery from the counsel area.

"Please don't grant her immunity," Mrs. Montgomery pleaded. "That other lawyer is right. She confessed to this. You can't just let her walk away."

Brunelle frowned. "If I don't, Karpati might walk free."

"We know," Mr. Montgomery said "But we don't want both of them to walk free."

Brunelle pursed his lips as he considered for a moment.

"She could still refuse to testify, you know," Yamata pointed out to Brunelle. "Just because she doesn't have a privilege to claim doesn't mean she has to say anything. She could just sit there and refuse to answer questions."

"What would happen then?" Mr. Montgomery asked.

"The judge would hold her in contempt," Brunelle answered. "And put her back in jail until she agreed to testify."

"Or until the trial is over," Yamata said. "The judge isn't likely to hold up the whole trial for this late gambit. If she can last another week in jail without testifying, the case will be over and she'll be released."

"That doesn't seem worth it," Mrs. Montgomery observed.

Brunelle had raised a finger to his pursed lips. "Actually, there's something even worse, I just realized."

"What?" Mr. Montgomery asked.

"If she does testify," Brunelle explained, "and says she did everything and Karpati did nothing, wasn't even there. I can't revoke the grant of immunity. She'd still walk. And most likely so would he."

"Mr. Brunelle?" the judge called out. "What is the State

going to do?"

Brunelle looked at Mr. Montgomery, Mrs. Montgomery, and Yamata in turn. Yamata frowned and shook her head. Brunelle agreed.

"Nothing, Your Honor," he announced as she stepped back to his table. "We're done with Miss Sandholm. No immunity."

Then, under his breath, "Damn it."

Brunelle tapped on his legal pad and frowned as the bailiff went to collect the jury.

"You know," Welles leaned over and whispered to him, "you could still call that fake Holly of yours. You know, the one you unethically sent into the jail to entrap my client?"

Brunelle looked out of the corner of his eye at his opponent but didn't say anything.

"I won't even object to the late notice," Welles went on. "Just tell me her name."

Brunelle finally turned to face Welles, and in so doing noticed that Karpati was looking at him as well, pen at the ready over his own legal pad.

"You want her name?" Brunelle asked.

Welles smiled. "Only to be properly prepared, I assure you."

Brunelle nodded thoughtfully. "How about initials?"

"Better than nothing," Welles replied.

They all stood as the jury entered the room. Brunelle raised a hand to block his mouth from the jury's view. "F.U."

CHAPTER 35

The next morning found Yamata in Brunelle's office. Brunelle hung up the phone and sighed.

"Chen says they're gone," he reported. "All of them, just vanished."

"Every last No Blood?" Yamata confirmed. "I thought they were supposed to be tough? Stand their ground or guard their turf or something."

Brunelle shrugged. "I'm sure if it were a rival gang, they'd still be there, spoiling for a fight. But when being around means getting picked up on a subpoena and helping the Man put one of your brothers in prison? Guess not."

"So what do we do?"

Another shrug. "We hope Chen can scrape somebody up while we're in court today. We're running out of witnesses." Then he recalled who the morning's first witness would be. "You ready?"

Yamata smiled. "Oh yes. Let's see what the good doctor has to say."

***

"Kat Anderson. Assistant Medical Examiner."

She identified herself for the jury with a pleasant smile, being sure to turn and address her responses to the jurors, not Yamata, who would be asking the questions. The decision to have Yamata do the direct exam had been easy. Yamata needed the experience examining a coroner.

And Kat was still pissed at Brunelle. The last thing they needed was Brunelle asking to have the M.E. declared a hostile witness.

"Are you familiar with the autopsy of Emily Montgomery?" Yamata began.

"Yes," answered Kat. "I performed it myself."

"Let's begin at the beginning then," Yamata directed. "What is the purpose of an autopsy?"

Kat nodded and turned again to the jury box. "The purpose of an autopsy is to determine the manner of death."

Yamata checked off the questions on her notepad. "And what are the possible manners of death?"

"There are four," Kat answered. "Natural causes, accident, suicide, and homicide."

"Were you able to determine the manner of death of Emily Montgomery?"

Again a look to the jury. "Yes."

Yamata nodded. "And what was the manner of Emily's death?"

"Emily Montgomery's death was a homicide."

Although expected, this response elicited a confirmatory ripple through the jury. But Brunelle knew it wouldn't be enough.

There was no real question that it was a homicide. 'Homicide' just meant being killed by someone else. Self-defense and lethal injection are homicides too, but they're legal. The real question was whether it was murder—*unlawful* homicide. And if so, did Karpati do it?

"Thank you, doctor," Yamata continued. "So the manner of death was homicide. What was the cause of death?"

"The cause of death," Kat answered, "was cardiac arrest brought on by an acute loss of blood."

"And were you able to determine what caused this loss of blood?"

"Yes," Kat replied to the attorney, then turned to tell the jury, "The only injury to the body was a laceration to the neck, impacting the carotid artery."

Kat illustrated the location of the artery by pointing to her own throat, on the right side, just below the corner of her jaw.

"How large was the laceration?" Yamata asked.

"Actually, it was rather small. Just enough to open the artery."

Yamata nodded thoughtfully as she checked off another question and answer on her pad. "So did it appear to be expertly made?"

Brunelle expected an objection from Welles. 'Objection! Calls for speculation,' or something like that. But Welles ignored it; he didn't even look up from his note-taking.

"Well," Kat considered, "in my opinion, yes. The incision was large enough to open the artery and no larger. It's exactly the cut I would have made to sever that artery."

"And were there any other pre-mortem wounds to the body?"

Kat shook her head. "None."

Yamata paused as she turned a page. But really, the pause served more to signal a new, and important, direction in her examination. "Can you please explain the significance of the carotid artery?"

"The carotid artery leads directly from the heart to the brain." Again Kat turned to the jury and indicated locations on her own body. "It's the first place blood goes when it leaves the heart. You see, as blood travels through the body delivering oxygen, it also takes away waste products like carbon dioxide. When the blood gets back up to the heart, the carbon dioxide is deposited into the lungs to be exhaled and fresh oxygen is put into the blood. When the freshly oxygenated blood leaves the heart, the first place it goes is up the carotid artery to the brain."

"So in a way," Yamata translated, to make sure the jury got it, "that's the purest blood in the body."

Kat nodded. "I think that's a fair statement."

"So what effect would a laceration to the carotid artery have?

"Absent immediate medical care, it would be fatal. It's not a survivable injury."

"Would a person's heart continue to beat?"

"Absolutely," answered Kat, "and that's the problem."

Brunelle leaned back and watched. These two were feeding off each other perfectly. A glance to the jury box confirmed the jurors were interested too.

"Why is that a problem?" Yamata asked, even though she knew exactly why.

"As I explained," Kat told the jurors, "the heart pumps blood directly into the carotid artery. But if the artery is severed, the blood can't reach the brain. Instead, it would spurt out of the body with each heartbeat."

"And would a person die from that?"

"Absolutely." Kat confirmed. "In a matter of minutes."

Yamata set down her legal pad. "You saw Emily's body at the murder scene, is that correct?"

"Yes, that's correct."

"And she was suspended upside down, is that correct?"

"That's correct," Kat answered. "I assisted in lowering her body to the ground. She was already dead by the time I arrived on scene."

"Would being suspended upside down impact the rate of blood loss from incision to the carotid artery?"

"Yes, it would."

"Can you explain how?"

"Certainly." Kat again exposed her neck to the jury as she explained. "The heart is designed to pump blood throughout the body, including pumping up against gravity into the brain. Hanging a body upside down would only accelerate the blood loss through the carotid artery, as the heart pumped hard enough to defeat gravity, but really was being aided by it."

Yamata crossed her arms. "Can you estimate how long it took Emily Montgomery to die?"

Kat frowned in thought. "Based on her size and the amount of blood lost, I would say not more than five minutes."

Yamata nodded. She paused just long enough for everyone to wonder what her next question would be, so they were paying attention when she asked it. "Would she have felt the blood loss?"

"She would've felt every spurt of blood with every beat of her heart."

Brunelle stole a glance at the jurors to confirm at least some of them winced at the thought. They did.

"Doctor," Yamata continued after a moment, "you've been

to a large number of death scenes, is that correct?"

"I've been to literally thousands of death scenes," Kat replied.

"How many of those," Yamata asked, "involved a significant loss of blood?"

"I would say most of them," Kat replied. "Gun shots, stab wounds, industrial accidents. Those can all involve a significant loss of blood."

"And where is that blood usually found, doctor?"

"It's usually found at the scene," Kat nodded. "Under, on, and all around the victim.

Yamata stepped to the projector and flashed a previously admitted photo of the crime scene up on the courtroom's screen. "Was there any such blood at this death scene?"

"No," Kat confirmed what the photograph showed. "There was no blood at all."

"How is that possible?" Yamata pretended not to know.

"Well," Kat explained to the jurors, "given the amount of blood loss and the location of the injury, blood would have been spurting out of her body with every one of Emily's heartbeats. The only explanation for the lack of blood is that the blood was collected as it came out of her body."

"And then removed from the scene?"

"Precisely."

"Thank you, doctor," Yamata nodded to Kat. "No further questions."

She sat down next to Brunelle and they both looked over at Welles. The defense attorney took a moment to stand up. He slowly set down his pen. He carefully smoothed out his suit. Then, facing the jury more than Kat, he asked that same damn question, almost like he was bored with it himself.

"You have absolutely no information that connects my client to this murder, isn't that correct, doctor?"

Kat let the smallest smile creep into the corner of her mouth. "Oh, I wouldn't say that, Mr. Welles."

Everyone in the courtroom looked up. Welles' record of witnesses answering 'No' had been perfect up to that point. Which just made Kat's response that much more amazing.

It surprised Brunelle. It surprised Yamata. It surprised the jury. It even surprised the judge. But most importantly, it surprised Welles.

And it was never good for a trial attorney to be surprised.

Brunelle knew, every trial attorney knew, that one ironclad rule of cross examination: 'never ever ask a question you don't already know the answer to.' The number two rule was never, ever ask an open-ended question. Lead, lead, lead.

But when you're surprised, sometimes you don't think straight. Sometimes you forget the rules. Especially when everyone in a crowded courtroom is staring at you.

"Why would you say that?" Welles stammered at the doctor.

Brunelle saw the grimace on Welles' face as he finished the question and realized what he'd done.

"I'm glad you asked that," Kat smiled. "Allow me to explain."

"Your Honor, I'd like to withdraw the question," Welles tried.

Yamata immediately stood up; it was her witness. "The witness should be allowed to complete her answer."

Judge Quinn smiled down at the defense attorney. "You asked the question, counsel. I'm going to allow the witness to answer it."

And she did.

"I was there when the body was lowered down. It took three of us: me and two patrol officers. And that was working *with* gravity. In addition, Emily's hands had been bound behind her back prior to death, and the rope was only removed post-mortem. I know it was removed post-mortem because the rope left impressions and blanching that would have dissipated if her heart had still been pumping blood at the time of removal. Based on those two things, I know that whoever was responsible for Emily's murder was strong enough, first, to overpower her and tie her hands behind her back, and second, to hoist her body from the ceiling."

"I fail to see how that implicates my client directly," Welles sneered. "There are plenty of people strong enough to do that."

"Then let me finish," Kat replied with a sharp, sweet smile. "I don't just cut open bodies. I am tasked with determining the cause of every death in the county. Often, the most valuable information comes not from an autopsy the next morning, but from the eyewitnesses the night before. As part of my investigation I reviewed every police report generated in this case. Every one. I know a young woman named Holly Sandholm witnessed the murder. And I know there's no way she was strong enough to overpower Emily or hoist her still struggling and very much alive body from the balcony by her ankles."

Kat paused and nodded toward the defense table. "But your client, Mr. Karpati, is strong enough … and that's exactly what Holly said happened."

Welles narrowed his eyes. "And do you always take the word of a teenage girl?"

Anderson shook her head and laughed lightly. "Oh, no. I have a teenage daughter myself."

The jury laughed too. *Perfect*, thought Brunelle.

"I know not to believe anything until I can confirm it," Kat continued. "I'm a pathologist, a scientist. And I'm telling you that what Holly told the detectives is wholly supported by the indisputable physical evidence. So when you asked me that there was absolutely nothing connecting your client to the murder, well, the answer is no, just the opposite. Your client had the strength and opportunity to commit it, and that's corroborated by the only witness."

Kat thought for a moment. "Well, the only *surviving* eyewitness."

Welles just stared at her for several moments.

"Wanna ask me another question?" Kat grinned.

Welles smiled too, but a cold, hateful smile. He turned and stepped back to his table. "No, thank you, doctor. No further questions."

Yamata jumped up to press her advantage, but Brunelle grabbed her arm. "No questions," he whispered.

"What?" she whispered back. "but—"

"The judge won't let us," Brunelle explained. "It's one thing if a defense attorney steps in it. It's another to let us elicit rank hearsay. And anyway, we don't need to. She killed him. Let it lay as is."

"Any redirect examination, Ms. Yamata?"

Yamata hesitated but only for a moment. "Er, no, Your Honor. Thank you."

"The witness is excused," the judge announced. "We'll take our morning break now. Please reconvene in fifteen minutes."

Once the jury filed out, Brunelle walked up to Kat as she stepped down from the witness stand. "I love you."

"Shut up," she laughed. "I'm still mad at you."

"I said I was sorry."

"You also said you wouldn't do it," Kat reminded him.

"What I said was," Brunelle raised a finger, "she wouldn't wear a wire."

Kat crossed her arms. "Really? You're sticking with that?"

Brunelle grinned. "Words matter."

"And talk is cheap."

"Okay, let me make it up to you."

Kat shook her head. "Good luck with that."

"Dinner. This Friday. My treat."

Kat hesitated

"Come on," Brunelle encouraged. "What's the worst that can happen?

"The worst that can happen is I give you a second chance."

"Parker's Grill?" Brunelle pressed on.

Kat raised an eyebrow. "That pretentious, overpriced place? You can't afford that on your government salary. I should know. Make it Jordan's."

"That's not much cheaper," Brunelle observed.

"Hey, Sherlock," Kat tapped him on the forehead. "I just said yes."

"You did?" Brunelle beamed. "Hey, how about that?"

"Yeah, Lizzy's still grounded for pulling that stunt for you," Kat explained. "So, she can stay home and watch TV while her mom gets a free dinner."

"Hardly seems fair if it's bought by the same guy who put her up to what got her grounded."

"Are you arguing against the date you had to talk me into?"

Brunelle shook his head forcefully. "No, ma'am."

Kat put her hands on her shapely hips. "Ma'am?"

"I think I better shut up now.," Brunelle said.

"I think you're right," Kat laughed. "See you Friday, David."

Kat strutted past Brunelle and out of the courtroom. He

watched her the whole way, then turned back to his surroundings, a boyish grin still on his face. But the grin drained away when he noticed two things.

Karpati still at the defense table, displaying a grin of his own.

And the word scrawled in large block letters on his legal pad:

'LIZZY'

CHAPTER 36

The break was over soon enough and Yamata came back into the courtroom wearing a frown. Brunelle knew she had stepped out, but hadn't known where she'd gone to. The bathroom, he figured.

"Bad news," she announced in a low voice as she reached him. "Chen's had no luck scaring up any No Bloods. And he says he's done looking for today."

Brunelle knitted his eyebrows together. "Why?

"Triple homicide on Capital Hill. Messy. The whole major crimes unit is there. Suspect got away, so if Chen's not at the scene, he'll be on the manhunt."

"Damn." Brunelle frowned and tapped his lips. He looked at the clock. It wasn't even eleven o'clock yet. "We're out of witnesses for today."

Yamata nodded. "We're out of witnesses for the trial," she

said. "Unless you want to start calling random patrol officers to stall."

Brunelle shook his head. "No. 'What did you do?' 'I put up crime scene tape.' 'What did you do?' 'I kept the log everyone signed in on.' No, we want to finish strong."

Yamata nodded. "Dr. Anderson was strong."

Brunelle nodded, but was still frowning. "Not strong enough."

"All rise!" Judge Quinn retook the bench.

"Are we ready to proceed?" she asked.

Brunelle grimaced. He forced a smile and gestured amicably up to the judge. "Well, actually, Your Honor, no. The State is having a small witness problem."

Judge Quinn looked at the clock. "Do you want to adjourn until after lunch?"

"I'd like to adjourn until tomorrow," Brunelle countered, then readied himself for the reaction.

The judge just raised an incredulous eyebrow. But Welles went into full drama mode. He smelled blood.

"Tomorrow?" he gasped. "I object. No, I do more than object. I protest. This is absolutely outrageous. The State has utterly failed to produce any evidence that my client was involved in this murder, let alone that it was done to advance his standing in a secret society of vampires. And now that they have reached the end of their case, they ask for one more day? The court should deny the request and force the State to rest its case."

The judge raised the other eyebrow at Brunelle.

"It's just one more day, Your Honor," he assured the judge.

Judge Quinn rolled her head back to Welles. "What's one more day, counselor?"

"What's one more day?" Welles repeated, aghast. "It's one

more day my client is held illegally. It's one more day my client is denied his freedom. It's one more day the government uses its power to trample upon the liberties of a God-fearing, law-abiding citizen."

When Judge Quinn seemed ready to question him on that particular description of Arpad Karpati, Welles pressed on. "We all know that as soon as the State rests, I will make a motion to dismiss the case for failing to present any evidence that connects my client to the murder. And we all know that when I make that motion, the court will grant it, and Mr. Karpati will be a free man. What's one more night, you ask? One more night is a travesty of justice, and nothing less."

"What about Dr. Anderson's testimony?" the judge tested.

Welles smiled sardonically. "You mean the testimony that was allowed after I withdrew my question? Well, apart from being an automatic appeal issue, her answer was rank hearsay. Although it may have been admissible to explain her scientific conclusions, the jury is not allowed to consider any statements by Miss Sandholm for their potential truth. My client was never able to cross examine Miss Sandholm, and therefore allowing the jury to consider her alleged statements as if she had actually testified would violate my client's right to confront his witnesses. I would expect the court to instruct the jury to disregard the statements for whether they are true or not, and limit their consideration only to explaining why the good doctor drew the conclusions she did. With that limited use, they also do not tie my client to the murder. And the court will grant my motion."

The judge looked back at Brunelle. "Counsel?"

Brunelle shrugged. "He's right, Your Honor," Brunelle conceded. "Dr. Anderson's statements were allowed to support her conclusion, not to admit Holly's statements without having her testify. But I disagree that the court would necessarily grant a motion to dismiss at this point. But either way, it's premature. We haven't rested yet and we need an adjournment until tomorrow morning."

Judge Quinn pursed her lips and nodded. "I will give you until tomorrow morning, Mr. Brunelle."

"Thank you, Your Honor," Brunelle replied.

"But Mr. Welles is right," she went on. "If you have no witnesses ready, you will rest your case. And if you rest your case as it stands right now..." she frowned, "...I will grant a motion to dismiss."

She stood up. "Court is adjourned until tomorrow morning at nine a.m."

The judge exited to her chambers and the attorneys packed up their belongings. Welles flashed a confident smile at Brunelle and Yamata, both of whom failed to offer any smile in return. Instead they walked into the hallway and waited in silence for the elevator.

When it came, they were the only ones on board. As the doors closed, Yamata asked, "Now what?"

Brunelle shook his head. "I don't know."

But, in truth, he did.

CHAPTER 37

"You have to testify," Brunelle said. He tried to make it sound more statement than plea.

"You know I can't," came the reply. "And you know why."

"What I know," Brunelle answered, "is that if you don't testify, he walks."

A shrug. "That's your problem, not mine."

Brunelle frowned and nodded. He put his hands in his pockets and turned to leave. "You keep telling yourself that," he said. "Especially when the next girl dies."

CHAPTER 38

The clock read 9:04. Judge Quinn was giving them extra time, Brunelle knew, but he also knew time had pretty much run out. Yamata came back in the courtroom from the hallway for the sixth time in as many minutes. Still no witnesses in the hallway, but this time Chen stepped in behind her. Any hope Brunelle might have had in seeing him was extinguished by Chen's shrugging shoulders and shaking head.

"Sorry, Dave. I got nothing."

"You look like hell," Brunelle observed. Chen had obviously been up all night. Brunelle hoped he'd found the other killer, but he would have preferred him finding a witness. Still, he knew his friend had done everything he could. "Not your fault, Larry. Maybe I can convince her not to dump the case."

"All rise!"

It was 9:05.

Quinn took the bench and her gaze immediately found Brunelle. "Is the state ready to call another witness?"

Brunelle stepped forward from the door to the attorney area. "Unfortunately, the State has no further witnesses, Your Honor."

He couldn't help but glance at Welles who was already standing up and displaying his asshole smile.

"Ordinarily, Your Honor," Welles trumpeted, "I would ask the state to rest in front of the jury. However, under the circumstances, that would seem to be a waste of time. As soon as Mr. Brunelle formally rests, we will move to dismiss the case. Your Honor has already indicated the likelihood of that motion being granted. Perhaps we could bring the jury out afterwards to explain what happened."

Judge Quinn looked to Brunelle. "Do you want to rest in front of the jury or not?"

Brunelle scanned the court room. The Montgomerys were in the front row. Duncan was in the back row. Edwards was by the door. And no one was coming in that door.

Still, insisting on resting in front of the jury would buy him some time. It would take several minutes for the bailiff to march them in, have Brunelle say the magic words "The state rests", and march them out again. Maybe he could use that time to manufacture an argument against dismissal.

"I'd like to rest in front of the jury, Your Honor."

Quinn frowned but nodded. "So be it." Then she instructed the bailiff to fetch the jurors.

They filed in and took their seats. Judge Quinn looked down at Brunelle.

"Does the state have any more witnesses?"

Time was up. Brunelle looked around the courtroom. He tried to ignore the knot in his stomach. He'd let down the

Montgomerys. He'd let down Duncan. He'd let down Yamata. He'd let down Chen and in a way even Edwards.

But he'd fought the good fight. He hadn't given up. Sometimes you give your best and still lose.

"Your Honor." he sighed, "the State re—"

The door to the court room smashed open.

"Is this room 120?" demanded the shapely brunette in the doorway.

"Faust," whispered Brunelle.

"Fuck," hissed Karpati.

"Finally!" announced Faust. "You wouldn't believe how much trouble I had finding this stupid courtroom."

Brunelle smiled and shook his head. "The state calls Debra Thompson to the stand."

"Objection!" Welles even hit the table as he jumped to his feet. If yelling 'objection!' was like telling the jury 'ouch'—and every trial lawyer knew it was—then hitting the table was like crying on top of it and asking for your mommy. "The State was about to rest."

"Close only counts in horseshoes, Mr. Welles," the judge replied with the slightest grin. She turned to Brunelle. "Was this witness on your witness list, counsel?"

"Yes, your honor," Brunelle was relieved to answer. "She was mentioned in the reports we provided Mr. Welles prior to the bail hearing."

The judge nodded. "Then you may proceed."

Faust cat-walked through the courtroom to the witness stand. As she brushed past Brunelle, she whispered, "Just don't ask what we were doing when I told you everything."

Brunelle managed a poker face and quickly began his direct examination. "Please state your name for the record."

"Debra Thompson."

"Do you go by any other name?"

Faust smiled and tipped her head slightly. "People call me Faust."

A slight chuckle rippled through the jury box and mister computer guy scooted forward in his seat.

"How are you employed, Miss Thompson?" Brunelle continued after a moment.

Faust turned and directed her answer to the jurors. "I'm a bartender at Darkness."

"Is that a tavern?" asked Brunelle.

"No," Faust smiled, "because it's not 1644. It's not a tavern; it's a night club."

More light laughter from the jurors. A polite smile from Brunelle.

"How long have you worked there?" he asked.

She shrugged. "Long enough."

Brunelle nodded and crossed his arms. At least the jury wouldn't think he'd coached her.

"Okay." He decided to move on. "Are you acquainted with the defendant, Arpad Karpati?"

She paused, then offered a soft, "Yes."

She didn't look at Karpati, but everyone else did. And he was trying to stare a hole right through her. Sometimes the best evidence is how a defendant conducts himself in court.

"How do you know Mr. Karpati?"

"He's a regular at Darkness," Faust answered. "Or he was anyway."

"When was the last time you saw him there?"

The answer was direct. "The night he murdered that girl."

"Objection." Welles smacked the table again. *Ouch, ouch, ouch.* "There's been no foundation for this witness's outlandish claim that my client was in any way involved with the unfortunate death of that young lady."

Judge Quinn looked down at Brunelle. "Can you lay some foundation, counselor?"

"I'd be happy to, Your Honor." He turned back to Faust. "How do you know he murdered her?"

Faust cocked her head slightly, with an almost puzzled expression on her beautiful face. "Well, duh. He told me."

And that, Brunelle knew, was the end of Welles' motion to dismiss. It's not hearsay if it's the defendant's own statements. It's evidence.

Brunelle nodded and paused before his next question, allowing Faust's testimony to sink in on the jury

"Let's back up." he said. "How often would you see Karpati at Darkness?"

Faust considered for a moment before answering. "Like I said, he was a regular. Not every night, but more nights than not."

"Was he associated with any particular group?" Brunelle still needed to prove the aggravator.

"Objection!" *Ouch.* "Calls for speculation."

"Lay some foundation first, Mr. Brunelle," Judge Quinn instructed.

"Yes, Your Honor," Brunelle nodded. He raised a hand to focus Faust's attention. "This is a yes or no question. Were you aware whether Mr. Karpati was a member of any particular group?"

Faust nodded crisply. "Yes."

Brunelle returned the nod. "And *how* do you know?"

Another full-lipped smile. "He told me."

Brunelle let himself exhale. Welles couldn't object anymore. Anything his client said could be used against him. Even to a bartender.

"And what did the defendant tell you about this group?"

Faust frowned for a moment in thought, then answered, "They called themselves 'No Bloods' and claimed to be vampires."

Again, a murmur rippled through the jury box.

Brunelle stopped and thought for a moment. Faust hadn't given him a lot, but it was what he needed and it was enough. He'd survive the halftime motion now. And the jury already knew Karpati was guilty; now they'd be allowed to render the verdict.

He could take Faust back to the beginning. Circle through her testimony again to make sure the jury heard and understood all of it. Flesh out the details. Expand it to its full potential.

Or not.

"No further questions."

Brunelle quickly sat down next to Yamata.

Faust had given him what he needed and he had no idea what else she might say. Best to shut up before any damage was done.

The good news was that Welles wasn't totally prepared for the abrupt ending to Brunelle's direct exam. He shuffled some papers together and stepped a little too quickly to the bar opposite Faust.

"Ms. Thompson," he started. "You claim my client confessed the murder to you?"

Brunelle knew Welles was flustered. That wasn't a well-worded question. It gave Faust too much room.

"More like bragged about it," she answered.

Welles' eyes narrowed a bit. "You're just a bartender, aren't you?"

"I'm not 'just' anything," Faust replied.

That was perfect. Especially for the jurors who were more

bartender like Debra Thompson than lawyer like William Harrison Welles.

Welles realized his mistake too. "What I meant, Miss Thompson, is that you aren't a friend or confidante."

Faust considered. "I'm not a friend, but I'm a bartender. Pretty sure that makes me a confidante. Especially after a few drinks."

Welles tapped his pen against his legal pad. He was only bolstering her credibility.

"Well, you must hear a lot of stories then, is that right, Ms. Thompson?"

Faust smiled. "Oh, yes."

"Do you believe everything you're told?"

Faust shrugged. "Depends on who's doing the telling."

Brunelle smiled. She was doing great. Welles wouldn't want to ask the next question, but if he didn't the jury would wonder why. Or worse, know why.

"What if Mr. Karpati is doing the talking?"

Faust nodded. She looked down thoughtfully. She took a moment to consider her answer. "I always believed Arpad."

Welles was in the hole. Brunelle wondered if he'd stop digging.

"And why is that?"

Nope.

The comfortable smile Faust wore disappeared. "Because he doesn't talk much. But when he does, when he tells me something, something bad, I believe him. I learned to believe him. He said he raped Holly Sandholm and sure enough, he did."

The jury box and the gallery exploded with gasps and whispers. Welles' eyes bulged in the sockets. Yamata gave Brunelle's arm an 'I can't believe she said that' bump. And Brunelle just stared up at the witness who had saved his case.

"Your Honor," Welles finally said after regaining himself. "I'd ask the court to strike the last answer as nonresponsive."

"Objection," Brunelle said quietly.

"Sustained," Judge Quinn said. "You asked and she answered. Ask your next question."

The hole was deep. More questions about Holly were probably only going to make it worse. Brunelle hoped Welles was flustered and angry enough to push forward, but Welles gathered his papers together and stepped back to counsel table. He looked like he was about to sit down. When he opened his mouth to speak, Brunelle thought he was going to say, "No further questions."

Not quite.

"You don't believe Mr. Karpati is actually a vampire, do you?"

Faust almost chuckled at the question. "No."

Welles returned the chuckle. "In fact, you would agree, wouldn't you, Ms. Thompson, that anyone who thinks he's a vampire would have to be crazy?"

Faust considered for a moment. "Yeah, I guess so."

"Thank you, Ms. Thompson." Welles nodded up to the judge. "No further questions."

"Mr. Brunelle?" asked the judge. "Any redirect?"

Brunelle considered. Welles hadn't really done any damage. He could try to expand a bit on some areas, but he could just expand it in closing. If he didn't ask any more questions, then Faust would be done and walk out the door.

And she hadn't even once used the phrase 'fucked from behind.'

"No further questions, Your Honor. Thank you."

The judge thanked and excused Faust. As she walked by

Brunelle, she offered the smallest wink. Brunelle ignored it, save his racing heart.

"Any more witnesses, Mr. Brunelle?" The judge asked.

Brunelle stood. "No, Your Honor. The State rests."

Judge Quinn nodded, then looked to the jury. "Ladies and Gentleman, that concludes the State's evidence. You are adjourned until tomorrow morning. The attorneys and I will stay in session to discuss scheduling. Thank you."

The bailiff escorted the jurors into the jury room. When the door closed, the judge looked down to Welles. "Motion denied," she said. "Any reason you can't give your opening statement first thing tomorrow morning?"

Welles forced an apparently gracious smile. "None, Your Honor. Thank you."

"Will you be ready to call witnesses as well?"

"Not only will we be ready, Your Honor, we will relish it."

This time it was Quinn who forced the gracious smile. "Wonderful, Mr. Welles. Then if there's nothing else, court is adjourned until tomorrow morning."

The judge left the bench and Brunelle exhaled a huge sigh of relief.

"That was lucky," Yamata whispered to him as they gathered their pads and papers.

"Sure was," Brunelle replied. "But we're not out of the woods yet."

"No, Brunelle," Welles interrupted, "you certainly aren't. See you tomorrow."

CHAPTER 39

"Thank you." Brunelle was leaning against the alley wall when Faust stepped through the backdoor at closing time.

If she was startled, she didn't show it. "I told you not to thank me for something I wanted to do."

"You didn't want to do that."

She shrugged. "I didn't want to not do it, and him walk. I don't need that guilt."

Brunelle nodded and they started walking toward Faust's apartment.

"I really do think he'll hurt someone if he gets out again," Brunelle said.

"I know he will," Faust answered. "He's a psycho. No, if he's out, someone dies. Some young girl. And if I could have prevented that and didn't...?"

She stopped and looked at Brunelle, her soft features half-lit by a nearby streetlight. "You can be pretty convincing, Mr. Prosecutor."

Brunelle glanced down and rubbed the back of his neck. He couldn't help the smile creeping onto his mouth. He looked up. "Let me walk you home."

Faust smiled too, but more with her mouth than her eyes. "I don't think so." She stepped close to him. "I'm not the one for you."

Then she leaned up and kissed him. A deep, probing kiss with her hands in his hair. When she finished, she pulled away and looked in his eyes.

"The one you thought of just now," she whispered. "Go home and call her."

Brunelle didn't know what to say. Faust held his gaze and stepped back.

"She's asleep right now," he finally croaked.

Faust nodded. "The good ones are. Call her in the morning." She turned to walk away. "Good bye, old man."

Brunelle raised his hand as she walked away.

"Goodnight, beautiful," he whispered.

***

"Good morning, beautiful," Brunelle practically sang into the phone.

There was a pause before Kat responded. "David?" she confirmed. "Are you drunk?"

Brunelle laughed. "It's only nine in the morning."

Kat paused again. "You know that's a non-answer, right?"

"I'm not drunk," Brunelle assured. "I just wanted to call to say hi."

"Oh," Kat said. "Well then, hi."

"So we're still on for tonight?" Brunelle asked.

"Absolutely. Unless there's a last-second, emergency

autopsy. But honestly those can usually wait. It's not like they're gonna get better."

"Charming," answered Brunelle. "Maybe let's not talk shop tonight."

"What are we gonna talk about then?" Kat asked.

"I don't know," Brunelle said. "Maybe us."

"'Us'?" Kat laughed. "David, it's our first date."

"It's our second," Brunelle corrected. "Don't forget coffee."

"I'm not sure that was a date exactly," Kat argued.

"Technically, I think it was," Brunelle replied.

"'Technically?'" Kat asked. "You're going to go legal on me?"

"See? We're already talking about us."

Kat laughed. "Well done, Mr. Lawyer."

Brunelle laughed too, then got quiet for a few seconds.

"You okay?" Kat asked.

"Yeah," he sighed. "It's been a long trial."

"Almost done?"

"I think so. I don't think Welles is going to call many witnesses. We may even finish evidence today. Closing arguments on Monday."

"Well, then," said Kat. "It sounds like you could use a night out."

Brunelle smiled. "I guess so."

"Good luck today, David," Kat said. "Knock 'em dead."

"Ha ha," Brunelle groaned. "Medical examiner humor."

"You gotta have a sense of humor to do my job," Kat defended. "Yours too, I think."

"I suppose so," Brunelle said after a moment. "Anyway, I'm looking forward to seeing you tonight.

"Me too," agreed Kat.

"Bye, Kat."

"Goodbye, David."

Brunelle held the phone against his forehead for a few seconds. He looked at the clock. Quarter to nine. Time to head down for Welles' opening.

Brunelle hoped it would suck. He knew it wouldn't.

CHAPTER 40

"Justice," Welles began. He stood in the well before the jury box, palms spread. "Perhaps the highest human ideal. Love and kindness and charity—we all aspire to those, or at least we agree that we should. But justice, and the pursuit of justice, is such a high cause, such a high ideal, that it's what we expect the very Creator to deliver at the end of days. We here on Earth do our best to try to bring some justice to a world so absent of it sometimes. Justice is what we look to, to get us through the hardest times, when the worst possible things happen to the best possible people."

Welles paused and looked down at his feet solemnly.

"Emily Montgomery is dead. Murdered. In a terrible, almost unimaginable way. And we want justice. Her parents want it. The prosecutor wants it. You want it.

"And ladies and gentleman," he looked up, "believe it or not, I want it too.

"However, the State is seeking something other than justice here. The State is seeking revenge. Emily Montgomery is dead. And now the State wants to kill Arpad Karpati. Not because of what he did, but because they can't kill Holly Sandholm."

"Objection, Your Honor." Brunelle didn't like objecting—especially during an opening statement—but that went too far.

"Sustained."

"Holly Sandholm admitted to this murder," Welles continued. "Holly Sandholm is guilty of this murder. But Holly Sandholm is a juvenile, and the United States Supreme Court has said that juveniles cannot be executed."

"Objection again, Your Honor." Even when you don't want to object, Brunelle knew, sometimes not objecting signals you're admitting the other side's allegations against you.

"It's an accurate statement of the law, Your Honor," Welles defended.

"It's argumentative, Mr. Welles," Judge Quinn replied. "This is opening statement, not closing argument."

"Understood, Your Honor." Welles offered a slight bow. "I'll move on to the facts."

Of course he'll move on, Brunelle thought. He'd gotten to say what he wanted. Twice.

"The facts," Welles continued, "are these: Emily Montgomery was murdered. Holly Sandholm confessed. And the only shred of evidence the State gave you that my client was in any way involved was a desperate, last-minute witness—a bartender, no less—to whom we are supposed to believe Mr. Karpati confided in because, of course, all murderers tell their bartenders everything.

"The fact that this is the only witness to connect my client to the crime, and that she was called at the last possible second, shows just how weak and desperate the State's case truly is.

"Justice isn't just about avenging the victim. It's also about protecting the accused. Justice cries out that no one be punished for a crime unless the State, with all of its resources, can prove that crime beyond any and all reasonable doubt."

Welles stopped and pretended to think, as if his next point hadn't been rehearsed over and over in his bathroom mirror. "Actually I misspoke. They don't have to prove the crime beyond a reasonable doubt. They've done that here. There is no doubt Emily Montgomery was murdered. But before a man can be strapped to a gurney and heart-stopping poison injected into his veins, the State also must prove beyond any and all doubt that it was *that* man who was responsible for the crime.

"And that, ladies and gentleman, the State has utterly failed to do."

Brunelle considered objecting again at the appeal to emotion with the gurney crack, he even figured his objection would be sustained, but that 'ouch' goes both ways. And so does failing to produce evidence. So far Welles had attacked the State's case. Brunelle was curious if he'd ever explain what evidence the defense planned to put on.

"And to make matters worse," Welles continued after a dramatically thoughtful pause, "the State wants you to believe this murder was committed because Mr. Karpati is a vampire.

"Now, quite honestly, ladies and gentleman, I find that incredibly disrespectful to the memory of Emily Montgomery. She was murdered by a human being, not some imaginary monster. And again the only witness for this outlandish assertion is the attractive bartender to whom everyone tells their secrets.

"Ladies and gentleman, a criminal trial is not like a conversation in the dining room, trying to figure out which child broke the cookie jar. There are rules and there are burdens and they are there for a good reason. Indeed, the highest possible reason.

"Justice.

"The State wants you to believe that the only way Emily Montgomery receives justice is by killing Mr. Karpati."

Again Brunelle choked back an objection.

"But I tell you, the only way justice is done in this case is to hold the State to their burden and acquit a man against whom there is no evidence. In fact, ladies and gentlemen, I submit to you that there are only two possible conclusions from the State's evidence. The first is that they did not prove the charge and my client must be found not guilty. The other possibility, the only other possibility, is that my client believes he is a vampire, in which case he is clearly insane and must be found not guilty by reason of insanity."

A murmur of shock rippled through the courtroom. Brunelle looked at Yamata, eyebrow raised. She raised both of hers in return.

"I will tell you now, Mr. Karpati will not testify. He doesn't have to and he doesn't need to." Welles raised a hand and pointed at all the jurors. "And shame on every one of you who just thought that must mean he's guilty. The judge has told you before and she will tell you again: you may not hold my client's right to remain silent against him in any way. Now I know, it's human nature. We expect someone to deny the charges against him. But when the burden is on the State to prove the charges and they fail to do so, then a defendant not only *may* stand mute, he should. He must. And so he will.

"But you *will* hear from a witness. A witness who will respond to this allegation that Mr. Karpati is a vampire—or thinks he's one. Dr. Russell Orbst. He will explain, quite simply and without any doubt, that if you believe Ms. Thompson, the bartender, then you will also be required to return a verdict of not guilty."

Brunelle looked over at Yamata to offer a 'can you believe this?' eye roll, but she avoided his gaze. Instead she was looking at Welles, smiling. A big smile.

"For you see, ladies and gentleman, gone are the days when friends and family of crime victims banded together to bring vigilante justice to suspected wrongdoers. How many innocent lives were destroyed by such barbaric practices? No, we have a system now. A system with checks and balances. A system designed to vindicate the victim and protect the accused. A system designed, ultimately, to effectuate that highest of human ideals. And so, ladies and gentleman, after you hear all the evidence, you will not be convinced beyond any and all reasonable doubt that my client committed this murder. And you will acquit him, as you are supposed to.

"And when you do, it will mean one thing: Justice.

"Thank you."

Welles returned to his seat. Karpati clasped his arm and nodded an obvious thanks. Then the judge excused the jury for a brief recess before starting testimony. Once they were safely inside their sound proof room, Brunelle looked over at Welles.

"NGRI?" he asked. "Really? You want your guy to go the mental hospital instead of prison?"

Welles smiled. "No, I want him to walk out the door tonight. But short of that, I'll take the mental hospital. Their goal will be to cure him as quickly as possible, upon which event he shall be released. And," Welles' grin darkened, "I expect a speedy recovery."

Brunelle's own half-smile faded fully. He nodded with begrudging understanding, then turned back to his trial partner. While his smile was gone, hers was still in full blossom.

"What are you smiling at?" Brunelle asked.

"Russell Orbst," she answered in a low voice. "I know him from my days in civil practice. He's a total whore. He'll say whatever Welles tells him to say."

"That hardly seems like something to smile about," Brunelle observed.

Yamata's eyes twinkled. "It's not. But I know why he's doing criminal cases now. The civil bar figured him out."

"Figured him out?" Brunelle cocked his head.

"Yep," Yamata practically laughed. "You're gonna have fun with him on cross."

Brunelle looked over at Welles, all smug and glad-handling his murderous client.

He looked back to Yamata, his smile returning. "Well, good. I could use a little fun right about now."

CHAPTER 41

"Russell Orbst, Ph.D."

He looked every bit the expert professor. Neatly trimmed beard, and eyeglasses that Brunelle suspected had a prescription of zero. And he was clearly comfortable testifying. He responded to the questions from the lawyer by turning to the jury to deliver the answers.

"Could you please tell the jury your qualifications?" Welles invited.

Brunelle sat back and listened to the list of universities, degrees, and awards.

"Approximately how many times have you testified as an expert witness?"

"More than I can count," was the smug reply.

"But less than you used to," Yamata whispered to Brunelle.

The introductions out of the way, Welles moved directly to

the heart of the matter. "Doctor, have you had a chance to review this case?"

"Yes," he looked to the jurors. "I have."

"And was that done at my request?" Welles clarified.

"Yes, it was."

"Specifically," Welles continued, "did I ask you to form an opinion regarding vampires?"

Russell laughed casually at the obvious ridiculousness of the question. "Yes, you did."

"Now doctor," Welles became more serious in response to Orbst's laugh, "are you familiar with any cases of individuals actually believing they are vampires?"

Orbst nodded thoughtfully, trading his bemused smile for a clinical scowl. "Yes, I'm afraid I am. Such cases are more common than one might think. In fact, there is actually a clinical diagnosis for it."

"Is that right?" Welles asked as if he didn't already know.

"Yes," replied Orbst. "It's called, appropriately enough, vampirism."

"And what are the symptoms of vampirism?"

"There are several symptoms," Orbst began, "but not all of them need to be present for the diagnosis to apply. The main symptoms are delusions, paranoia, narcissism, and often insomnia. There are also documented cases of auditory and visual hallucinations. One also often sees a deep sense of persecution."

"Are you referring to individuals who want to be vampires?" Welles clarified, "Or who already believe they are vampires?"

"Well, both types exist of course," Orbst turned to direct his response to the jurors, "but the diagnosis I was referring to applies to those who actually believe they are in fact vampires."

"Do such people ever act upon this belief?" Welles asked.

"Do you mean do they bite people in the neck?" Again a comfortable look at the jury.

"Perhaps not the neck," Welles replied, "but yes, is there an attempt to drink human blood?"

Orbst frowned at the jurors. "Unfortunately, yes. Believe it or not, there are actually advocacy group for vampires. They fight what they consider misinformation about vampires. But even they claim a need for human blood. They just assert that the blood is obtained consensually by people who understand and support these true vampires."

"I imagine," Welles posited, "that such understanding blood-donors are rare."

"I would think so," chuckled Orbst. "Hence the neck-biting."

"Now these people who believe they are vampires," Welles steered the topic slightly, "they aren't really vampires, are they?"

"Umm, no." Orbst smiled at the jurors. "There are no such things as vampires."

"And believing yourself to be a vampire doesn't make you a vampire?"

"Believing yourself to be a vampire makes you mentally ill."

Welles smiled. "Would you go as far as to say that it would make you insane?"

Orbst pretended to think about the question. "Yes," he answered after a moment. "I would agree with that."

Welles took a moment to let the jurors get interested again. "Could you explain to the jury just what is meant by the word 'insane'?"

This time when Orbst turned to look at the jury, he opened his palms and took on a truly professorial affect. "People use the word 'insane' everyday, and they use the word 'crazy' and more colorful terms like 'nuts' and 'wacko.' In day-to-day speech, that's fine. We all understand it simply means something strange or out of the ordinary. But in the legal field, in a courtroom setting, insane has a very specific definition."

"And what is that definition?" Welles was practically salivating as he asked the question.

"A person is legally insane if he doesn't appreciate the wrongfulness of his conduct, if he is unable to distinguish right from wrong."

Welles nodded. "So why would someone who believes he's a vampire be considered legally insane?"

"If someone truly believed he was a vampire," Orbst explained, "then he would truly believe he needed human blood to survive. There is a principal in the law called necessity. There are times when it is lawful to kill someone. One of those times is when it's necessary to save your own life. A person who truly believed he was a vampire might truly believe he needed to kill another person in order to preserve his own life. He would be wrong, but he would still believe it. And that would make him insane."

Welles turned away from Orbst for a moment. When his back was fully to the jury he gave Brunelle a wink.

"Now, doctor, I'd like you to imagine the following hypothetical." Welles turned back to his witness. "A man who truly believes he's a vampire, and truly believes he needs the blood of young girls to survive, goes and murders a young girl to drink her blood. Would that person be insane?"

Again a pause for fake consideration. "Yes. Yes, that person would be insane."

"And if a person commits a crime because they're insane, can that person be found guilty of the crime?"

"No," Orbst turned and instructed the jury. "That person would be not guilty by reason of insanity."

"Thank you, doctor." Welles looked up to the judge. "No further questions. Your Honor."

Brunelle watched Welles take his seat at the defense table. Welles didn't wear his usual smug grin—not in front of the jury. But he didn't have to. His direct had been perfect. It planted the seed of doubt generally, without ever actually admitting Karpati committed the murder or really thought he was a vampire.

So it was Brunelle's turn to cast doubt on the doubt.

"Good morning, doctor. It is doctor, right?"

Not really, Brunelle thought.

"Yes," Orbst replied. He was undoubtedly used to the question, so kept his testiness in check, but Brunelle knew it still bugged him. "I have a PhD in psychology."

"Okay, but you're not a medical doctor?"

"I don't need to be. I have five years of advanced studies in human psychology and behavior. Knowing how to perform ankle surgery wouldn't make me any more qualified."

So, not too testy, but definitely close to the surface. Yamata was right. Good.

"Do you have a practice then?" Brunelle asked. "Patients you see on a regular basis?"

Orbst turned again to deliver his answer to the jury. "My expertise is forensic psychology, not clinical. I conduct research, write articles, and of course, testify in court. I don't maintain a list of clinical clients on top of that."

"So you make your living testifying?"

Orbst took a moment to reply, wisely considering the question. "I make my living as a forensic psychologist. Testifying is just one of the aspects of that."

Brunelle nodded. Then he gestured toward Orbst. "Nice jacket."

Orbst seemed taken aback. "Er, thank you."

"Is that Lauren?"

"Uh, no," stammered Orbst. "It's an Antoni."

"Antoni," repeated Brunelle. "Is that a nice brand?"

Orbst shrugged. "Pretty nice."

Brunelle peered over the little wall in front of the witness stand. "Nice shoes, too. Are those also Antoni?"

"Antoni doesn't make shoes," Orbst replied.

"Your Honor," Welles stood up. "I'm going to object. I don't see how Mr. Orbst's fashion choices are relevant to the case at bar."

"I'm getting to that," Brunelle replied.

"Get to it quick, Mr. Brunelle," the judge warned. "Or move on."

Brunelle turned back to Orbst. "Your shoes are scuffed."

Orbst looked down. "Are they?"

"Well, more like the sole is paper-thin. And your jacket is fraying at the end of the sleeve."

Orbst raised an arm to examine the unwinding threads.

"Your practice or whatever has seen better days, I take it?"

"I don't have a clinical practice," Orbst reminded him. "And my forensic psychology business is doing fine, thank you."

"You don't get paid much for those articles you write, do you?"

"I get royalties."

"You can't live on the royalties."

"Well, no. Not exclusively."

"In fact, you make the majority of your income from testifying, isn't that true?"

"I am paid for my time." The standard answer. Time, not the

opinion. Really.

"In fact," Brunelle pressed, "you'll say whatever you're paid to say, isn't that right?"

Brunelle knew it was too soon to ask that question. Orbst had heard it a thousand times and would knock it down easily. But then Orbst would think he'd won the exchange and relax.

"Of course not. I am a professional and have a reputation to maintain. A psychologist who would just say anything would soon lose all credibility."

Brunelle nodded, hand to his chin. "Good point, good point. I mean, you want to be the kind of witness who gets hired again and again, right?"

"Consulted, not hired," Orbst corrected. "And yes, exactly."

"You haven't been testifying in criminal cases very long, have you?"

Brunelle saw Orbst tense up at the question. He hoped the jury noticed it too.

"I've testified in criminal cases for some time now," Orbst answered coldly.

"But before that," Brunelle continued, "you mostly testified in civil cases, isn't that right? Lawsuits, malpractice, divorce and child custody? Stuff like that?"

Orbst nodded carefully. "Yes, stuff like that."

"And in that kind of a setting, you might get hired by either side to testify, correct? Husband or wife? Patient or hospital?"

"Correct."

"And then you screwed up, didn't you?"

Orbst's face hardened. "I didn't screw up. I testified honestly and the judge made a decision."

Brunelle smiled. Yamata was right. Orbst still wasn't over it. "You testified that a man was mentally fit to raise his children, then he drowned his daughter in the bath tub."

"I testified honestly and accurately about a forensic psychological opinion. The court made a decision based on all of the evidence in the case, not just my testimony. That little girl's death is not on my head."

The force of his denial belied it.

"And after that," Brunelle went on, "no one in the civil law community wanted to hire you again, isn't that right?"

"That is not right. I continued to testify in child custody cases and all types of civil litigation."

"But word got out, and the phone stopped ringing and you needed to expand into criminal work to pay the bills?"

"I chose to expand into criminal work."

Brunelle nodded again. "But criminal work is different, isn't it? The prosecution, we have our own psychologists, right? The doctors at Western State Hospital, right? And they're paid a salary. We don't have to pay them anything. So the State never would retain a private psychologist like you, isn't that right?"

"I wouldn't say never," Orbst replied. "It does happen."

Brunelle smiled. "But you'd agree that it's very rare."

Orbst surrendered a shrug. "I suppose it is rare."

"Exactly. So if you're going to make a living testifying in criminal cases it's going to be by testifying for defense attorneys, isn't it?"

Orbst pulled himself up. "It's going to be by testifying truthfully."

"Sure, sure." Brunelle waved the answer away. "But you would agree with me that if every time you got hired by a defense attorney, you testified that the defendant was competent to stand trial and legally responsible for his actions, well, after a while, those defense attorneys would stop calling?"

"I, I don't know."

"But," Brunelle drew the word out and laid a hand on the witness partition, "if you testified in a notorious murder case—one with shock value from an innocent young girl and a crazy vampire-man—and the murderer got acquitted because of your testimony? Your phone would be ringing off the hook, wouldn't it?"

"I testified honestly," Orbst defended.

"Those shoes are really scuffed," Brunelle observed. "Have you bought a pair since Lindsey's dad drowned her in the tub?"

"Objection!"

"Do you think of that little girl when your finger catches on a loose thread of your jacket?"

Welles objected again, but the judge wasn't ruling on them, so Brunelle pressed on.

"Exactly how many zeros is your so-called expert opinion based on?"

"My expert opinion is based on years of study and hard work, a thorough review of all the police reports, and an extended clinical interview with Mr. Karpati!"

Brunelle stopped. He turned to Yamata who raised an eyebrow to show her understanding. Welles' eyes flew wide, then dropped intently to his legal pad. The judge had the slightest curve buried in the corner of her mouth. The jury didn't get it. But they were about to.

"You spoke with Mr. Karpati?" Brunelle asked.

Orbst's face showed he realized it too, but it was too late.

Anything you say can and will be used against you.

When Orbst hesitated, Brunelle clarified, "You spoke with him about the murder?"

"Objection," Welles tried half-heartedly. "Calls for hearsay."

Weak. Every lawyer in the room knew a defendant's own

statements were never hearsay when the prosecution elicited them.

"Overruled."

"Then another objection," Welles tried again. "Any communications between my client and his psychologist are privileged."

Weak too.

"He opened the door, your honor," Brunelle responded. "The witness mentioned the interview first, not me. I should be allowed to explore."

"Objection overruled. Proceed, Mr. Brunelle."

Brunelle mentally cracked his knuckles. He'd just wanted to rattle Orbst, make him look like the expert-for-hire he was. He hadn't expected this, but he wasn't going to waste it either. The temptation was to ask 'What did he say?' But this was cross examination. Lead the witness, make him agree with you.

"Karpati admitted he killed Emily Montgomery, didn't he?"

Orbst shifted uneasily in his chair. He absently fondled the worn cuff of his jacket. Finally, after the gears stopped turning, he looked away from the jury and admitted, "Yes."

All the professionals in the room knew Orbst would never get hired again. Too bad for him.

"He tied her hands behind her back, hoisted her upside down, and slit her artery to drain her blood, right?"

Another pause. Orbst still didn't look at the jury. "Right."

"And he did it because he wanted people to think he was a vampire, correct?"

Orbst looked up at Brunelle defiantly. "He did it because he is mentally ill and not responsible for his actions."

Brunelle frowned. One question too far, that was the danger in cross. But he'd needed to ask that question. Having done so, he had to clean up Orbst's answer. Or at least scare the hell out of the jury so they would never consider walking Karpati.

"Mentally ill?" Brunelle confirmed.

"Yes," Orbst sneered. "It is my expert opinion that Mr. Karpati suffers from vampirism and therefore does not appreciate the wrongfulness of his conduct. He believes it necessary for his survival, and therefore acts under the influence of an irresistible impulse."

Brunelle nodded. "Irresistible impulse?"

"Oh yes."

"So given the opportunity, he'd do it again?"

"Absolutely," Orbst crossed his arms. "And when he did, it would prove I'm right."

Brunelle nodded. There was so much more he could ask, but he was done.

"No further questions."

"Redirect examination, Mr. Welles?"

All eyes turned to the defense attorney. He was in a heated whisper exchange with his client. Whatever Karpati was saying, he was angry and emphatic. Welles was shaking his head and tapping the legal pad with his pen for emphasis.

"Mr. Welles?"

Welles stood up. "No further questions, Your Honor. Thank you. At this time the defense would suggest we adjourn until Monday. My client and I have some matters to discuss."

The judge shrugged and looked at Brunelle and Yamata. "Any objection?"

Brunelle looked to Yamata, but she waved her hand back to him. His call. It had been a long week. And it was a good way to leave it with the jury.

"No objection, Your Honor."

"Court is adjourned," the judge quickly declared. "We will

reconvene Monday morning at nine."

The clerk hit the gavel, the bailiff led out the jurors, and the guards took Karpati away. Brunelle expected a smarmy comment from Welles, but the defense attorney was busy packing his things. He avoided Brunelle's gaze.

"That was awesome!" Yamata yanked Brunelle's face to hers. "I could kiss you right now."

Brunelle stared at her for a second, then shook his head. "How the hell did you win a sexual harassment suit against your old firm? You're the most flirtatious lawyer I've ever had the pleasure to try a case with."

Yamata cocked her head, then let out a belly laugh, just making her even hotter somehow. "Is that what everyone thinks? No wonder no one will talk to me. Not 'sexual harassment,' dummy. 'Sexual discrimination.' As in 'gender discrimination.' As in one of the old-boy partners got caught saying he'd never make a woman a partner. Thought he'd hung up his phone but it was on speaker. Hello, payday, and goodbye, law firm. Finally could pay off my student loans and take a kick-ass prosecutor job for half the money."

Brunelle was stunned. That was a lot of unexpected information all at once. He latched onto the last bit. "Half?"

Yamata laughed again, a deep purr of a laugh. "Okay, a third." Then she thought for a second and laughed again. "Hey, don't tell anybody, okay? I kinda like everyone being scared of me."

Brunelle shrugged. "I won't tell, but Welles probably heard and I can't speak for—"

He turned to the defense table, but Welles had slipped away without so much as a goodbye. That wasn't like him.

Brunelle should have known it meant trouble.

CHAPTER 42

"And then he says," Brunelle swallowed his bite and pointed at Kat with his fork, "No, my opinion is based on my education, the police reports, and.... my interview of Mr. Karpati!"

Kat nodded. "Okay, sounds reasonable."

Brunelle shook his head. "No, no. The point is, we didn't know he'd done that interview. Defense doesn't have to share that with us. I mean, not unless they're gonna use it at trial. Welles probably should've given it to me, but I never would have known if Orbst hadn't let it slip."

"Ah," Kat nodded. "Well, lucky break for you."

"Luck?" Brunelle scoffed. "More like scathing cross examination."

Kat just raised an eyebrow.

Brunelle laughed. "Okay, yeah, luck. But I got him to admit that Karpati had confessed to the murder."

"Wow, how did he explain that away?"

"He said Karpati was mentally ill and driven by an irresistible impulse. He'd do it again and that just proves he's not guilty by reason of insanity."

Kat's face scrunched into a frown. "That logic is what's crazy."

"I know," Brunelle laughed. "And so does the jury. No way they let him out."

Then his cell phone vibrated. He looked down at it and shrugged. "I'm gonna ignore that, I think."

"What if it's a new homicide?" Kat questioned.

"Then you're probably the next person they'll call," Brunelle smiled. "We'll see if your phone goes off too."

The persistent hum of Brunelle's phone was clearly audible over the voices of the restaurant.

"You know," Kat leaned onto the table and gestured toward the phone on his hip. "That could be fun under the right circumstances."

Brunelle smiled. "Hmm. Not sure I can text one-handed."

Kat's eyes twinkled. "Maybe I'll do the texting. You can watch."

Brunelle's eyebrows shot up. "Oh my." Then he scanned the restaurant. "Time for the check, I think."

Kat laughed. "We're still on the appetizer, Romeo. Besides, Lizzy's at the house."

"I have an apartment," Brunelle replied. "And we can hit the drive-thru on the way back to your place."

"Great, walk in to see my daughter, still smelling like you and french fries. Mom of the Year."

Brunelle's phone was still buzzing, or rather buzzing again.

Kat nodded at it. "You better answer that."

Brunelle frowned. "Yeah, you're probably right."

He pulled the phone from its hip holder and pressed it to his ear. "Brunelle." Then. "Hey, Michelle. What's up? Kinda busy here."

Kat waited and watched as Brunelle's face dropped.

Then he lowered the phone. "Karpati posted bail. He's out."

He thought for a moment then raised a haunted gaze to Kat. "Lizzy."

"Lizzy?" she repeated quizzically. Then her voice hardened. "What about Lizzy?"

"He knows it was her," Brunelle explained. "That she's the one I sent into the jail. He overheard us talking after you testified."

Kat stared at him for just a moment, then screamed, "Damn you, David Brunelle!" and ran for the door.

Brunelle only hesitated for a second before running after her, his hand digging the car keys out of his pocket as he went.

CHAPTER 43

The front door was kicked in, the door frame splintered by the deadbolt. No young accomplice to trick the girl inside into unlocking it.

Brunelle stepped in carefully and scanned the scene, cursing himself for never buying that gun his detective friends kept telling him he needed, handling the cases he did. "Lizzy?"

But Kat pushed past him. "I'll check the bedrooms, you check down here." She was practically to the top of stairs by the time she finished the sentence. A second later she was out of sight around the corner.

Brunelle stepped through the house, trying to listen for a clue as to where they might be. There had clearly been a struggle. Drawers pulled open in the kitchen. Someone looking for a knife most likely. But had it been Lizzy for defense, or Karpati for...?

He shook his head. He needed to stop analyzing it like a

crime scene.

This wasn't Emily; it was Lizzy.

"Mmmph!"

Downstairs. The family room. Brunelle dashed down the stairs and pulled up short at the landing.

Lizzy was on her stomach, her hands tied behind her, her mouth gagged with a towel. Karpati was kneeling on her back, a steak knife in his hand and a gleam in his eye.

"Why, hello, Mr. Brunelle. Welcome to my acquittal."

Brunelle swallowed hard. Even if he lunged, he could never reach Karpati before he sliced Lizzy's throat.

"Acquittal?" Brunelle said. "Looks like count two to me. Attempted Murder."

Karpati smiled broadly. "Didn't you hear Dr. Feelgood today? A second murder proves I'm insane. I get away with murder by committing a new murder. How crazy is that?"

When Brunelle didn't respond, Karpati laughed again. "Get it? How crazy is that? Crazy. Get it?"

Brunelle nodded. He looked at Lizzy. Her eyes pleaded the words her mouth couldn't. Karpati's knife was less than an inch from her own carotid artery. Karpati had dispensed with the formality of the bucket. It would be enough just to kill her.

"Look, Karpati," Brunelle raised his hands but made a point not to step toward him, lest he get spooked and slash Lizzy's throat right then and there. "This won't work. A second crime never excuses the first. We can charge them together, then they're cross-admissible. Even if we don't seek death, you're looking at twenty years mandatory minimum on each count, no good time. That's forty years. You're twenty already, so best case is you're sixty when you get out. But drop the knife and this is only an attempted murder."

Karpati shook his head and actually pressed the knife against Lizzy's throat. She whimpered but couldn't move away from the blade. "You're not listening, Brunelle. Murder to get away with murder." Then Karpati grinned. "And you know the best part?"

Brunelle shook his head slowly. "No," he said. "What's the best part?"

"You picked the victim for me," Karpati chimed. "This is the bitch you sent into the jail to trick me, right? Your girlfriend's daughter? Perfect. I mean, I would have been willing to kill any little bitch, but you— You helped me decide exactly which little bitch to filet."

Brunelle swallowed again, this time against the bile rising in his throat. "Great."

He decided to press on. Lizzy was still alive, that was something. "Listen, Karpati, really. You don't have to kill her. Let me explain. Dr. Feelgood said it was an irresistible urge. You being here proves that, right? So you don't actually have to kill her. I stopped you. The end. Attempted murder is as good as actual murder for that."

Karpati nodded. "Okay, yeah. I see what you mean. Sure." He nodded some more and looked down at the helpless girl he was straddling. "There's just one problem."

"What's that?"

"I *want* to kill her." A rough laugh and another wide-eyed grin. "Say goodbye to your step-daughter, Brunelle."

Two gunshots echoed off the walls. Karpati flew backwards off of Lizzy and Kat stepped out from behind Brunelle, a wisp of smoke trailing up from the muzzle of her .45 semi-auto.

"God, you lawyers talk a lot."

She stepped over and untied her daughter, who clasped her,

sobbing.

Brunelle stepped over to Karpati. One shot to the chest. Potentially survivable. The one that removed the top of his head, not so much.

"Huh." Brunelle shoved his hands in pockets. He looked over to Kat and Lizzy, still embracing, then back at what was left of Arpad Karpati. "I guess I won't be giving that closing argument on Monday after all."

EPILOGUE

"Holly pled guilty, huh?"

Chen was sprawled out in one of Brunelle's office chairs, gazing out the window at the sun setting over Elliot Bay.

"Yep," Brunelle confirmed. "As soon as she heard Karpati was dead, she insisted on pleading. We actually reduced the charge to conspiracy to commit murder. Saved her some time."

Chen turned back to Brunelle. "Why'd you do that?"

Brunelle shrugged. "She was a victim too. No way she participates in that murder without Karpati controlling her. She seemed truly remorseful, In fact, she could barely get through the guilty plea because she was sobbing so hard."

Chen nodded. "Well, that's probably a good thing."

Brunelle returned the nod. "Yeah, she'll have to live with Emily's death for the rest of her life. There's more than one type of punishment."

Chen frowned thoughtfully. "You think so?"

Just then, there was a rap on Brunelle's door frame. It was

Kat, dressed for a night on the town. "Ready for the ballet, David?"

"Ballet?" Chen laughed.

Brunelle shrugged. "I rest my case."

THE END

The following is a preview of

TRIBAL COURT

the next David Brunelle legal thriller

Available Now!

CHAPTER 1

"Don't you hate it when the victim kinda deserved it?"

Seattle Police detective Larry Chen crossed his thick arms under his police-issue raincoat and looked to his friend for a reply. Dave Brunelle, King County homicide prosecutor, didn't look up from the dead body splayed at their feet. Instead he nodded and pushed his hands deeper into his own raincoat—thrown on at one in the morning when he got Chen's call.

"Just try not to say that on the stand," he said.

The murder victim was a man, late forties, overweight, and most definitely dead. His blood glistened black in the cracks between the cobblestones of Founder's Park in Seattle's Pioneer Square district. He was on his back, arms sprawled, shirt cut away by the same paramedics who left behind the adhesive chest pads they'd used to attempt resuscitation despite the multiple stab wounds to his chest. The rain was coating his face in droplets that trickled into his ear and the folds of his neck. He lay at the base of the plaza's 56-foot totem pole, like an offering to the spirits represented in the carvings, their faces made all the more grotesque by the forensic team's floodlights and the red and blue strobe of the cop cars clogging the narrow streets surrounding the square.

"So why did he deserve it?" Brunelle asked, more concerned with the potential jury nullification issues than the justness of the man's death. "Was it self defense?"

"No," Chen was quick to answer. "Witnesses said there was an argument, but nothing physical until the killer pulled out the knife and stuck it into our guy's chest."

Chen extracted his notebook from his damp pocket. "It's not what he did. It's who he was."

Brunelle finally looked up from the corpse. "Who was he?"

"George Traver," Chen read from the latest page of his running notebook. "Child molester. Registered sex offender. Failed to update his registration six months ago. Last known address was a trailer down near Tacoma. Had a warrant out for that, plus two more for shoplifting and drunk in public."

"Ah," replied Brunelle, wiping some rain from his nose. "Still, not exactly worthy of a knife in the chest."

"He was the suspect in two more child luring and indecent exposure cases."

"Okay," Brunelle agreed. "That might do it. Kind of a community service killing, huh?"

"Exactly," Chen confirmed.

Brunelle peered around the plaza. It was almost closing time. Intoxicated gawkers stumbled past the crime scene tape trying to get a glimpse of what lay at the base of the totem pole. "So where was he living?"

"He was homeless," Chen answered. "Sleeping on benches downtown mostly."

"Probably why he didn't register," Brunelle observed.

"Probably," Chen agreed, "although they're allowed to

register as 'homeless.'"

Brunelle frowned. "I always thought that was stupid. It kind of defeats the purpose."

"Sure does."

"So, who's our suspect?" Brunelle asked. He needed a suspect before he could get involved. Unsolved would mean no defendant to charge. "Another homeless guy?"

"Nope, the homeless guys liked him," Chen answered. "I sent two patrol guys to interview some of them. Most scattered, but the few who stayed said ol' George here was a great guy. Salt of the earth."

"I'm sure," Brunelle scoffed. "What's the suspect description?"

Chen looked down at his notepad. "Male, twenty-something, Hispanic or Native."

"Wow, not very helpful," Brunelle observed. "That describes about twenty-five percent of the people in Pioneer Square tonight."

"Maybe," Chen shrugged, "if you include Hispanics. But if you limit it to Natives, then it's probably one, maybe two percent."

It was Brunelle's turn to shrug. "And if we reduce it to Native men with one testicle and a prosthetic elbow, we can really start to narrow it down."

Chen cocked his head at his friend. "One testicle?"

Brunelle threw up his hands. "I'm just saying, you can always narrow it down. Why would you limit the description just to Natives if the witnesses said Native or Hispanic?"

Chen looked down at the lifeless body before them. "Our victim is Native."

Brunelle pursed his lips. "I don't see why that matters. It's not like murder stays in one race. If somebody killed you, I wouldn't assume the murderer was Chinese."

Chen smirked. "You should. If I wind up murdered, you can be pretty sure it was my wife."

"Oh yeah?" Brunelle laughed.

"Yeah," Chen laughed too, but it faded and he shoved his hands in his pockets. He pushed a foot out toward the dead man splayed out at the base of the totem pole. "You gotta know someone to hate them enough to kill them."

A set of fingernails dug into Brunelle's back. "Hey there, Mr. Brunelle," came a sweet female voice from behind him. Assistant Medical Examiner Kat Anderson had arrived. She pulled her nails down the length of Brunelle's back as she walked past him. "Long time, no call."

Brunelle stiffened at the voice, then relaxed slightly as she passed him and knelt next to the corpse. He knew she was right. "Yeah," he offered. "Sorry about that. Been busy."

She turned and smiled at him. Her smile held warmth, but other thoughts too. "Of course you have. Me too."

She returned to her examination of the murder victim. She wore a long raincoat that covered her curves, but the hood was pushed back, leaving her black hair and soft face exposed to the rain. He supposed her knees were getting wet and cold from the rain-drenched cobblestones. He remembered the last time they'd really talked and he regretted not having called her since then. Their last case together had ended badly. Or at least, it had almost ended badly, and he'd been reluctant to draw Kat, or her daughter, into danger again. He knew he'd been distant for the right reasons; he just didn't know if she knew it.

"A-hem," Chen cleared his throat. Then he took Brunelle by the elbow. "Why don't we step over here and discuss next steps."

Brunelle looked up sharply, then nodded. He allowed Chen to lead him toward the street. "Right. Next steps. What are the next steps?"

"The next steps are you stepping away from her while she does her job," Chen said. "I thought you two were an item or something, but it sure doesn't seem like it now."

Brunelle shrugged. "I think maybe we were going to be, but I haven't followed up. I don't like what happened on the Karpati case. I don't want to let that happen again."

Chen looked over his shoulder at Anderson. She had pulled on her latex gloves and was palpating the corpse's neck. "I'm pretty sure she can take care of herself."

Brunelle looked too. He sighed. "Yeah, I know."

"Maybe this has more to do with you," Chen started, but before he could say more, Anderson stood up and stepped over to them.

"No mysteries here," she announced as she pulled her gloves off. "Two stab wounds. One to the stomach, ruptured his small intestine. That would have been survivable, with prompt medical intervention, but the second one was directly to his heart. I'll need to do a full autopsy to determine where exactly it struck, but he was dead as soon as the blade went in."

"Sounds intentional," Brunelle replied.

"Maybe even premeditated," Anderson answered. "Murder one?"

Brunelle allowed a grin. "That's what we'll charge. Just don't let Larry on the stand. He thinks it's justifiable."

Anderson cocked her head at the detective. The motion sent rain drops cascading off her thick hair. Brunelle wished he hadn't noticed, and pretended the sight didn't send his heart racing.

"Justifiable?" she asked.

Chen shrugged. "Community service killing. Guy was a child molester."

Anderson frowned. She looked back at the body. "Did I say murder? I meant suicide. Obvious suicide."

Brunelle shook his head and laughed. "Great. Lead detective says it's justified and the M.E. says it's suicide. No way I get a conviction now."

"Lighten up," Chen slapped his back. "You need a defendant first anyway. Hopefully one that's even worse than ol' George there."

Just then a patrol officer hurried over to them. "We located the suspect," she announced. "Down on Alaska Way. Still had the blood on his hands. They're taking him to the precinct right now."

Chen turned to Brunelle. "You coming to watch the interrogation?"

"Wouldn't miss it for the world," he answered, both relieved and saddened to have an excuse to escape from Kat.

# # #

THE DAVID BRUNELLE LEGAL THRILLERS

Novels

Presumption of Innocence

Tribal Court

By Reason of Insanity

A Prosecutor for the Defense

Short Stories
(available exclusively for Amazon Kindle)
Case Theory

Beyond a Reasonable Doubt

ABOUT THE AUTHOR

Stephen Penner is a prosecutor and author from the Seattle area. He writes a variety of fiction, including thrillers, mysteries, and children's books.

His other works include the paranormal mysteries *Scottish Rite* and *Blood Rite*, the science fiction thriller *Mars Station Alpha*, and *The Godling Club*, a young adult paranormal adventure. He also writes and illustrates the children's book series *Professor Barrister's Dinosaur Mysteries*.

For more information, please visit his website:
www.stephenpenner.com

RING OF FIRE PUBLISHING

www.ringoffirebooks.com

Printed in Great Britain
by Amazon.co.uk, Ltd.,
Marston Gate.